Warm Hands Cold Heart

Tracy L. Ward

Willow Hill House
Ontario, Canada

WARM HANDS COLD HEART

The Marshall House Mystery Series

CHORUS OF THE DEAD
DEAD SILENT
THE DEAD AMONG US
SWEET ASYLUM
PRAYERS FOR THE DYING
SHADOWS OF MADNESS
WARM HANDS COLD HEART

TRACY L. WARD

First Edition
ISBN: 978-0-9958914-7-0

Copyright © 2018 by Tracy L. Ward

Cover Art Copyright © 2018 by Jessica Allain

Edited by Lourdes Venard, Comma Sense Editing

All rights reserved. Except for use in any review, the reproduction or utilization of this work in whole or part in any form by any electronic, mechanical or other means, now known or hereafter invented, including xerography, photocopying, and recording, or in any information storage or retrieval system, is forbidden without written permission of the publisher.

This is a work of fiction. Any names, characters, places and incidents are either the product of the author's imagination or are used fictiously, and any resemblance to actual persons, living or dead, business establishments, events or locales is entirely coincidental.

WARM HANDS COLD HEART

For Caleb
you've had it in you all along, now it's time bring it to the light

TRACY L. WARD

Chapter 1

SCOTLAND, December 1868—The scream that escaped the girl was loud enough and shrill enough to send Margaret's innards into an uneasy vibration. Margaret's hand was trapped in her patient's vice-like grip as the young thing bore down hard, giving all of her might to birthing her child, who was suddenly desperate to join the world. For hours the girl had laboured, moving through each contraction with increasing agony as her pains progressed. For much of the afternoon and evening it looked as if the baby would never come, or at least would not come until next morning. The girl had scarcely dilated and Violet Bane, the attending midwife and founder behind Wendall Hall, had said it would be many hours before she and Margaret would be called upon to assist in the delivery. But hours shriveled into minutes when a routine check indicated the baby was coming and would not wait for Violet or even Margaret's husband, Jonas, to be summoned.

"I cannot do it, Mrs. Davies," Maisie pleaded, looking up through sweat-dampened tendrils of hair.

Margaret repositioned herself so Maisie could see her better and reaffirmed her grip of Maisie's sweaty palm. "You can do this, as millions of other women have since the dawn of time. Your body knows what to do. You just need to help it along a little, all right?"

A meager nod escaped Maisie, whose facial expression looked less than convinced by Margaret's attempts at reassurance. Maisie was barely fifteen, and scarcely over one hundred pounds. The girl was one of their highest-risk patients and her situation was made all the worse by the fact that no one paced for her well-being in the other room. No family members awaited news of her fate or that of her unborn child. Maisie would have laboured alone were it not for Margaret's close vigil and continued encouragement. In that dimly lit room, with only lamplight to illuminate them, it felt as if Margaret and her charge were the only two people in the entire universe.

"What if she doesn't come?" Maisie asked.

"She's been sent for, as well as Dr. Davies," Margaret said.

"Neither will get here in time," Maisie said, arching her neck, signaling that another contraction was building up inside of her.

"I'm here, Maisie," Margaret said. "I am not leaving you." She pushed back some wet strands of hair from Maisie's face and then ran a cold cloth over her patient's brow. "You have to let go of my hand. I need to check to see if the baby's crowning."

Reluctantly, the girl released Margaret's hand, finally allowing blood flow to Margaret's fingers. A quick glance confirmed the baby would be arriving with or without the presence of the midwife.

"All right, Maisie, this is what I want you to do..." Margaret pulled the stool beneath her and sat down, readying her hands to catch the baby. "When you feel that next contraction I want you to push with all your might, yes? Can you do that?"

"I don't think I have the strength."

"Yes, you do. God gave you this baby. He will give you the strength."

When Margaret turned her attention to the baby she fought the urge to look away. So much fluid, blood, and agony was proving difficult to get used to even after attending over a dozen births while at Wendall Hall. Marry that to the fact that a strong, healthy infant at the other side of things was hardly a guarantee. Women fought hard for the birth of their babies and some would never see the fruits of their labours as either mother or baby or both could find themselves no longer for this world. Women in labour were expected to toil and pray for the best of possible outcomes without knowing what providence had in store for them or their offspring.

This would be Margaret's fate as well. In a few short months she'd be the one wailing in agony on the bed, screaming for the pain and discomfort to stop. She'd be the one silently praying for the life of her child and perhaps her own as well.

Jonas, her husband, had not wanted her to take up such a position, not while she awaited the birth of their first child. He had warned her about the gruesome business of baby catching. "Not all your patients will survive," he had said.

"Do all your patients survive?" she quipped.

Margaret was certainly no shrinking violet. She had once aspired to enter medicine and did not see any great difference between a man's ability to handle life's unpleasant realities and a woman's. Violet Bane was proof enough of that and had been for over two decades.

Even still, Jonas had said the sight of childbirth would most assuredly make her more anxious for her own condition than she already was. He had been right to a degree. As determined as she was, Margaret hadn't been prepared for the messy business of birthing a baby, and she'd certainly never expected she'd be catching a baby all alone.

"Oh, is it almost over?" Maisie groaned through gritted teeth.

Margaret hesitated. The baby's head was protruding further and further out. The contraction subsided. "I don't know," Margaret said, against her better judgment. A quick glance to Maisie told Margaret that it hadn't been the most reassuring thing to say. "You can do this, Maisie. One more push, I think. Maybe two."

The door burst opened behind them and Violet Bane stormed in. She quickly removed her outer layer of clothing, sending flakes of snow cascading all about her. "I'm here, Margaret," she said, tossing her snow-frosted coat to the side.

Margaret jumped from the stool and made way for the midwife.

"How are we doing, Maisie?" she asked, as another contraction came forward. "Hold Margaret's hand. That's it. Bare down, now. Once you feel that urge, give it all the strength you've got. The babe's almost out. And one, two, three..."

Seconds later the familiar muffled cry of a newborn filled the room. Margaret watched as Violet held the child with one hand behind the head and another at its buttocks. The umbilical cord was still attached as she repositioned the baby at her chest.

"It's a girl, Miss Maisie," Margaret said, taking in the look of the bloody and sticky child. She reached for a cloth and went to the foot of the bed to help Violet clean her off.

"A girl." Maisie's voice denoted her quiet relief. The worst was over.

Margaret smiled as she wiped the blood from the baby's head. "A beautiful, healthy girl."

After a precursory examination, Margaret swaddled the baby and placed her in the bassinet with a large red Christmas bow adhered to the side in acknowledgment of the upcoming holiday.

"Can I hold her?" Maisie asked, positioning herself higher in the bed.

Margaret looked to Violet for permission. Sometimes it was best if the birth mother wasn't granted such permission. After twenty years as midwife at Wendall Hall, Violet had become quite the expert in detecting who among them were strong enough to hold their babies and bond with them for just a few minutes before placing them in the care of others. Some of the new mothers, if given the child for a minute or two, would refuse to let them go, reversing their earlier decision to give the babies up for adoption. Some even became violent at the notion of handing them over. Ultimately, before leaving Wendall Hall, all the women gave up their child, but things ran so much smoother if a certain amount of protocol was followed.

Violet must have thought Maisie was a low risk for violence or an emotional outburst. She gave a nod to Margaret, who gingerly brought forward the child.

"I'm going to name her Christina, on account of Christmas next week."

Violet gave a half smile. "I can tell ye, the adoptive parents may have already chosen another name for her."

"Oh, I know," Maisie said, looking down at the wee thing in her arms. "It's just for myself, I guess. I will always remember her as Christina."

Margaret was forced to turn away. The thought of giving up her own child sent a rush of panic throughout her stomach. She was barely halfway through her pregnancy and already she was prepared to protect Jonas's child with her life. She could never imagine her own flesh and blood being raised by perfect strangers. She couldn't bear the thought of never seeing it again, not after carrying it for so long and toiling for days to see it born. She ran a hand over her protruding belly and closed her eyes for a moment to calm herself.

Since beginning her work there she had to remind herself often that the women and girls who came to them hadn't the same position in life Margaret enjoyed. They had neither a husband at their side nor a safe home to which to take their newborn. Their only luxury was that of finding out about Wendall Hall so that they might receive health care in the last days of their pregnancy and know for certain their child was going to a home, to be part of a family and not be subjected to the whims and lack of care more often found at baby farms and orphanages. The babies born at the hall were given the best possible chances in life, oftentimes better than if they remained with their birth mothers.

"Are you all right, Margaret?" Violet asked quietly. "Do you need to take a seat?"

"Yes, quite all right," she answered. She waved her hand at the matron's offer of a seat. "I can stand." Margaret looked over her shoulder to Maisie. "How soon will we know if she's contracted the fever?"

Child bed fever was the largest concern for post-partum mothers. Even the most uneventful births could end in tragedy when a woman developed a sudden fever and died.

"Did you wash your hands?" Violet asked.

"Yes."

"And everything which came in contact with our patient?"

"Yes, of course."

Violet smiled, pleased that her tutelage had made such an impression. "Then it seems the odds are in our favour. I have not lost a patient in four months, Mrs. Davies. There's no sense in trying to tempt fate now." Violet gave a wink and returned her attention to the patient in the bed.

"When will the couple get here?" Maisie asked.

"Not until the morrow," Violet answered with a soft smile.

"Perhaps Christina should stay with me until then,"

Maisie said, pulling the swaddling blanket tighter over the baby's shoulders.

"That isn't entirely wise," Violet said.

Maisie's expression fell. "I understand."

Violet did not take the child away immediately, though. She stood over the exhausted mother, looking down at her. "You are resolved to your earlier decision, yes?"

After a moment's hesitation, Maisie nodded. "I don't have any other choice. I'll lose my place and then neither of us will be fed or stand a chance at happiness." Maisie looked down at the child and reached over to touch the baby's plump, little chin. "I pray she does better than me," she said, her voice low. "I pray she'll not have to toil or suffer as I do."

As Violet received the baby, Margaret had to push aside a tear that spilled over onto her cheek.

"You would not be the first mother to offer such a prayer," Violet said as she turned and gingerly gave Margaret the baby. "See that she is brought to Mrs. Gibson and that she begins nursing straightaway. I'll examine Maisie and see that she is cleaned up."

Margaret nodded and headed for the door. She could hear Maisie's muffled cries even as she entered the hall. The noise continued for a number of steps. So sorrowful were those following few seconds when a recently made mother becomes a mother no more. Whether Maisie had no other choice or not, it was still the most heartbreaking moment of human existence, the worst Margaret hoped to ever witness. She doubted she would ever get used to the crying no matter how many times she was made a part of it.

☙ ❧

The nursery was a closed-off room, far from the dormitory, where a line of eight cots were arranged, four against each wall. The babies housed there were all meant for families, each one adopted and signed for before any of the mothers gave birth. Wendall Hall enjoyed a long waiting list of wishful adoptive parents, something Violet, the head matron, had worked tirelessly to establish. It was helpful to the adoptive families to know the babies were healthy, the mothers as well. Anyone associated with Wendall Hall could be assured of the high standard of care provided. It was a matter of pride for Violet but also a matter of principle.

The newborn Christina squirmed a little beneath her swaddling blanket as Margaret marched her toward the wet nurse, who had only just replaced another sleeping newborn to its cot.

"Oh, look at the wee thing," Mrs. Gibson said, pulling back the blanket with one finger to look at the new addition to the nursery. The wet nurse was a plump woman in her mid-thirties with five children of her own. Only her youngest, Luke, a six-month-old now sleeping soundly in a nearby cot, was permitted in the nursery alongside her. "She'll catch her death in this cold if we're not careful. So scrawny, she is."

Margaret allowed Mrs. Gibson to pull the babe toward her and then watched as the wet nurse took her to her seat nearer the fireplace. With the newborn no longer in her arms Margaret was reminded how small the child actually was. "Her mother has a small frame as well."

Mrs. Gibson looked up in surprise. "She has plans to keep her child, then?"

Margaret closed her eyes and shook her head, aware of her error. They called them birth mothers to differentiate them from the adoptive mothers who would come to pick up their babies. "My apologies," she said quickly. "I only meant—"

"I'ze knows what's ye meant," Mrs. Gibson said, saving Margaret from any further awkwardness. Within seconds and with only the slightest of coaxing, the newborn was suckling away thirstily. "There now," Mrs. Gibson said. She looked up to Margaret. "Take a seat, child," she said. "You look fit to evaporate if we ain't careful." She nodded toward a wooden chair not so far away.

When Margaret did finally sit down she realized how much she needed it. She closed her eyes against the pain in her legs and relished the sense of relief she felt.

"Tis not an easy thing," Mrs. Gibson said, "running 'round after birthing mothers. Not fer a proper lady the likes of you."

Margaret opened her eyes in surprise. Up until then

Margaret had thought she was doing a good job hiding her lineage from those she worked alongside. Only Violet knew who she truly was and where she had come from. "How did you know?"

Mrs. Gibson let out a huff. "Mrs. Davies, you ain't the sort of girl we get in here often. You speak properlike and have more manners than most. I can always tell." Her smile was warm and inviting, the sort of smile Margaret wished she would have when her children were older and seeking advice. "Sometimes we get bonny lasses in here from proper houses down south. They'ze in a motherly way, nowhere to turn, embarrassed to be at the doorstep. But they'ze always thankful. Always glad to return home, their families being none the wiser."

Margaret wondered at a few of her own friends she'd known back in London. Had they truly been leaving on extended holiday or were they actually headed here?

"They'ze seem to think they need to apologize for taking up a bed." Mrs. Gibson shook her head. "Violet has always made them welcome. All are welcome here."

"They pay for their care, don't they?" Margaret asked.

Mrs. Gibson nodded. "Oh, yes. Thems that can pay, plus a little extra, which gets used for thems that can't. It's how Violet keeps this place going, you see."

Margaret nodded. She did see. Wendall Hall was once a Scottish estate spanning thousands of acres. The building they sat in was over three hundred years old with creaky floorboards and stone walls throughout. A newer part of the building had been attached on the south side, facing the road. Only a ten-foot-long corridor connected the two buildings. The older portion housed the birthing rooms and nursery. The newer portion was where the expectant women spent their final weeks waiting for the first signs of impending birth. Two weeks was the longest anyone had ever needed to stay.

A low stone wall circled the immediate area around the house with a few wooden gates throughout. Beyond the wall was a barn building, a carriage house for the horses and other implements the groundskeeper used to keep up the property. Beyond the carriage house and down the hill were the cottages, once reserved for the married staff employed by the original owners, now occupied by a few of Wendall Hall's employees. Behind the cottages were the woods, spanning hundreds of acres before meeting with the town of Helmsworth, where Margaret and Jonas had recently taken up residence.

The property was secluded, with only the immediate locals aware of its true purpose. The women arrived here after hearing about it from others, those having heard of it in a similar fashion. And so on and so forth went the chain of information. Wendall Hall was never spoken of freely or acknowledged in any formal manner. Women would write to Violet seeking assistance and the head matron would send a trusted doctor or, on rare occasions, she'd head out herself for an initial assessment. From there she'd make them a reservation and they'd begin the task of finding the wee thing a home.

Mrs. Violet Bane, a widow for the better part of thirty years, had been running Wendall Hall since its founding. The property had been bequeathed to her by an aunt and not long after the women's charity had been born. She was a bit of a bluestocking, many would say, devoted to her work without the smallest inkling toward remarrying. It was rumoured Mrs. Bane preferred the company of women and had even had a devoted female companion for a time. Margaret had been warned, pulled aside during a tea welcoming her to the area. "She's very queer," one of the church society ladies had said. "Very queer indeed."

"What, pray tell, is so queer about her?" Margaret had asked. She had only met Mrs. Bane on one occasion and had found her nothing of the sort. Her question was met with a shrug but nothing more. Queer, it would seem, was enough of a descriptor for anyone who lived in the small village of Helmsworth. Queer was all she needed to know.

"I had no idea such a place existed until I arrived here," Margaret said, rubbing her round, pregnant belly more so out of habit than anything else. "I wish I had known about it months ago." She had been thinking about a friend, someone who could have used such a charity earlier in the summer.

"That's the hardest part," Mrs. Gibson said, adjusting the baby at her breast. "A few doctors know about us but they are less inclined to tell their patients. We wouldn't want to encourage wanton behaviour." Mrs. Gibson nearly laughed. "As if that were the only reason a woman falls pregnant and not because men force themselves on those that can't defend themselves." She cocked her head slightly sideways as if to indicate the petite-sized mother upstairs. "Mrs. Violet's had a difficult time getting the community to accept us and I'm not so sure they have entirely."

"Would they rather an increase in the amount of street children? Destitute poor?"

"Tell the truth, I don't know what they want," Mrs. Gibson said, lowering the now sleeping child from her chest. She quickly covered up herself and repositioned the swaddling clothes. "Some days they are happy enough that we keep to ourselves," she explained, "other days you don't know what sort of local madness is going to come marching up the laneway."

The wet nurse stood, placed the baby in the bassinet beside her, and then rolled the apparatus a bit closer to the stove.

Fannie Mae, another woman who worked there, passed by the open door in the hall in a hurry and then doubled back, most likely having seen Mrs. Gibson and Margaret seated opposite each other. "Did I miss it?" she asked, coming into the room.

Margaret smiled. "Only by twenty minutes," she said.

Fannie Mae let out a groan of disappointment. "I came as soon as I could," she said. Fannie Mae was a few years younger than Margaret, with reddish-auburn hair and pleasant disposition. She and Margaret had been fast friends, often found working side by side.

"Margaret managed it all on her own," Mrs. Gibson said.

"Not entirely," Margaret corrected her. "Violet arrived when it mattered."

Fannie Mae clapped hands together at the sight of the newest addition to the nursery. "Oh my word," she said, approaching the bassinet. "She's such a small thing!"

"Yes, and I just got her to sleep," Mrs. Gibson said, gently ushering her from the room. "If ye want to chat, and squeal, perhaps you should head to the kitchen and make Mrs. Davies here a tea. She's earned it."

"Of course," Fannie Mae said. "Come, Margaret, you can tell me all about your first birth."

Margaret found herself being ushered from the room. "It wasn't exactly my first birth," she said as they made their way down the hall. The kitchens were at the opposite side of the building and were most likely completely empty given the late hour.

"Don't be so modest," Fannie Mae said, slipping her arm into Margaret's. "Consoling a screaming woman deep in the pain of birth is not a simple task. All the hard work was done before Violet arrived."

"Well, I don't know about that," Margaret said. "I wouldn't know the first thing about catching babies. I'll leave that—"

Fannie Mae stopped and forced Margaret to stop alongside her. When Margaret looked she spied a black shadow at the end of the hall, large and looming.

"Which one of ye left the gate open to Tally's stall?" came a gruff voice from the darkness. It was Benson, Wendall Hall's caretaker, an overall cantankerous old man.

Margaret and Fannie Mae exchanged glances.

"It wasn't us, sir," Margaret said. She had never had any need to enter the carriage house or stables, not in the entire four weeks since she had begun her work there.

"I think it was me, sir," Fannie Mae said. "I'm sorry. Mama let me have the horse so I could get here quicker. I put Annabelle in the stall next to Tally's. I must have bumped the latch."

"Tally is an old one. She doesn't like open spaces. She must be confined." Benson walked toward them in his hunched-over manner, his ears nearly level with the tops of his shoulders.

"I understand, sir," Fannie Mae said, bowing her head slightly. "I was in such a rush to get inside."

"Next time, don't be!" Benson was directly in front of them now, his broad, imposing figure enveloping them in his shadow. Margaret could smell the man's putrid breath and the effects of the barn on his outer coat. He had been out driving Violet to Edinburgh and back and the chill of the winter air still radiated off him. He pushed through them, sending each to either side of the hall. "Ye be better to leave the mare hitched to the carriage and let me look a'ter her," he said as he made his way.

"I didn't know you were in there," Fannie Mae called after him.

"If my horse is in there, I'm in there," he said.

As he walked, his silhouette was swallowed by the darkness, the sconces on the wall doing little to illuminate the narrow hallway.

The women came back together slowly, as if an unseen force kept them apart until it too retreated down the hall after its master.

Fannie Mae gave an exaggerated shiver, shaking her shoulders and suppressing a playful smile. "How does he always manage to give me the creeps?" she asked. "Mama says there's nothing that man would rather do than see to those horses." They began making their way down the hall again. "And I do believe she's right."

"You'll have to make sure you close the gate next time," Margaret said, "or you'll find yourself forever on his bad side."

"I don't think he has ever had any side but a bad side. We are all doomed to remain on his bad side, I'm afraid. I dare say even someone as pleasant as you, Margaret." Fannie Mae laughed and slipped into the kitchen. Margaret followed close at her heels.

Chapter 2

Jonas arrived long after their second cup of tea. He blew in with a puff of snow before he was able to close the door behind him. Margaret heard his footfalls first and then his sigh of relief for having made it through the gauntlet of the winter's first significant snowfall. She popped up from her seat in the kitchen, where she and Fannie Mae had pulled chairs toward the fire, and met him in the hall.

"You made it," she said, smiling. They had been married nearly two months and she still could not stop herself from acting the giddy schoolgirl each time she saw him. For nearly a year, while they kept their attachment secret, she had had to act calm and almost indifferent when he was around, something which grew excruciatingly difficult to do. Their romance was a contentious one, forbidden from the start due to his lack of property or fortune and her family's abundance of them. He was the only son of a washerwoman and she the only daughter of the third Earl of Montcliff. They met because of Margaret's brother Peter, who had defied their father and attended the University of Edinburgh's medical school. While there, Peter met Jonas and the unlikely surgeons became fast friends. Despite his success as a surgeon, Jonas was never a likely match for Margaret, who was destined to marry a member of the peerage, or at the very least, someone whose prospects included more than a tidy living dressing the wounds of the inflicted. The divide between their situations never seemed to matter, however, and probably did more to drive them together than keep them apart.

Now, despite the objections of her family, Jonas Davies, professor at the University of Edinburgh, was her husband by law and choosing. She may have had to leave her entire life behind in London to be with him but, if asked, she'd wholeheartedly admit to being the happiest she had ever been in her entire life.

"Did I make it in time?" he asked, disentangling himself

from his scarf and outer layers of clothing.

Margaret shook her head. "A baby girl was born nearly an hour ago," she said.

Fannie Mae came to the kitchen door and leaned into the frame. "Can I fetch you a cup of tea, Dr. Davies?" she asked.

"Tea would be lovely but"—he glanced to the door—"there's quite a bit of snow coming down and if we have any hope of making it home we ought to get started soon. As long as Violet no longer requires your service, of course."

"Are the roads so bad?" Margaret asked, walking to the window to have a look for herself. She couldn't see much beyond the lantern affixed to the wall outside the door. Large flakes of snow patted the window of the door, clinging together and obscuring the view.

"Tis not the roads we need to worry about," Jonas said. "Arthur was headed further on to Haddington this evening so he left me at the lane. We'll have to walk the path through the woods to get home."

There were apologies hidden among his words of explanation, an apology for not having the means to own a carriage and team of their own, an apology for not having the sorts of luxuries Margaret had been raised with, and an apology for now expecting her, the sister of the fourth Earl of Montcliff, to walk the better part of three miles to get to their rented cottage in Helmsworth.

Margaret smiled. "Then I will be enjoying your full attention for the next hour or two," she said, coming toward him. Ignoring the snow that was now melting and dripping from his hair, face, and coat, Margaret pressed both her hands into his chest and looked up at him expectantly. "Sounds like a lovely way to spend an evening."

Jonas very nearly blushed before he bent down to plant a kiss on her cheek. "If you are no longer required here, we ought to get going before the snow gets deeper."

Fannie Mae was first to head down the hall to the cloak closet. "I hope you dressed warmly," she said, opening the door next to the kitchen.

Margaret met her inside. "Warm enough, I think."

Fannie Mae had grown up in Helmsworth, the small town stuck in the shadows of nearby Edinburgh. She was

Scottish through and through. She knew the winters well and she was able to predict a forthcoming wind, a significant snowfall, or an early spring. Jonas and Margaret possessed no such skill. Despite being raised in Edinburgh himself, Jonas was a city rat, never having left the confines of Old Town for the greater part of his formative years. He was better equipped to predict the train schedules than he was equipped to predict the weather.

"The snow on the ground will help you find your way somewhat," Fannie Mae said, helping Margaret secure her cloak at her neck. "Nothing as dark as the woods in summer but in winter the snow will reflect some of your lantern light," she explained. "The path between the trees should be easy to follow," she continued, pulling Margaret's muff from the shelf above. "I don't think I need to warn you about staying together," she said.

"I should hope not," Jonas said from the door.

"Will you be here again in the morning?" Margaret asked.

Fannie Mae nodded. "I'm going to help Mrs. Bane tend to Maisie for the next while, though I do hope she just sleeps, and then I'll take Annabelle home. I'll be back the usual time, I suspect."

Margaret nodded. "Very well. I shall see you after breakfast then."

They shared a quick embrace before Margaret turned to her husband.

"Ask Benson for a lantern or two," Fannie Mae called out from the door as they left the building, "if you can convince the old goat to part with one."

Margaret couldn't stop herself from laughing as Fannie Mae's words found her in the snowy dark. She knew she shouldn't tease her elders but it was only in good fun and it wasn't as if he didn't deserve the reputation. His anger toward them had stayed with her for some time after he had left and even now, with her husband at her side, she hoped they'd not encounter him again.

They found the outbuilding latched shut but illuminated. A number of lanterns hung from the wooden building's rafters and wood block pillars. Further in, horses whinnied and huffed against the cold. Margaret doubled-checked Tally's stall gate while Jonas searched for Benson.

"He was just inside not an hour ago," Margaret said. "Perhaps he's gone to his cottage."

"Do you think he'll mind if we take one of these?" Jonas asked, gesturing to one of the glass-sided lanterns already aglow. "There's a number of them here," he said. "I can't see how he will miss this one."

Margaret had no desire to get on Benson Fraser's bad side. She had avoided it for the most part. She imagined if he were going to be particular about anything it would be the very thing Jonas and she thought would have little consequence. But, without a lantern to light their way through the snow, they'd surely get lost. Not seeing any alternative, she nodded and Jonas pulled it down from its hook.

After securing the carriage house doors, Margaret pulled her cloak tighter and looked to the gate. Something had moved out of the corner of her eye.

"What is it?" Jonas asked, lifting the lantern and following the direction of her gaze.

"I saw something," she answered. After keeping an eye on the area a few seconds more she forced a smile and turned away. "Must have just been the snow playing tricks," she said.

They followed the footpath down a slight embankment at the back of the carriage house and crossed the open field to the edge of the woods. The path through the trees was not yet completely covered by snow but Margaret had no doubt it soon would be if the snowfall continued at the same rate. After only ten minutes in the open her cloak looked more white than its intended emerald green. Jonas too was completely covered and could easily be swallowed by the surrounding landscape if he chose not to move.

At the edge of the trees Margaret looked back at the house. She expected to see Fannie Mae at the window, waving perhaps, but there was no sign of her. A few windows gave off light, lamps in use among the various rooms, which served as a beacon in the wintry weather.

"It will shine so much brighter next week when all the candles are lit for Christmas Eve," Margaret said as she turned back to Jonas. "I'll have to make a point of coming out this far to have a look."

They walked through the trees side by side thankful for the very little snow that had made its way down from the canopy. A few inches of snow were much easier to walk in than the four times as much that accumulated out in the open.

"I was helping the vicar and the Presbyterian men's group hang wreaths on the village lamp posts when I received your message," Jonas said. "The main road through town looks quite lovely now with big red ribbons on each of them."

"Oh, how delightful," Margaret said with almost girlish excitement. "Are we going to get a tree? I realize it's not much of a tradition here but I do wish to be reminded of home. Please say yes. Mother began the tradition for us as children and I'd very much like to do the same for ours."

"Our children? Meaning more than one?"

"Of course," Margaret said, slipping her arm through her husband's and repositioning her muff. "I imagine we will have half a dozen children before long."

"Half a dozen!"

Margaret laughed. "I'm only teasing," she said. "But I do wish for a goodly number, three, maybe four. Think of it, Jonas. Think of all the Christmas mornings we will have with our robust little ones."

The look on Jonas's face remained doubtful.

"You want to say something but won't because you don't want to alarm me," Margaret said. "I am determined to have a marriage that was better than my parents, and that means you must tell me what you really think, even if you believe it will make me angry." She waited, eyeing him sideways as he struggled. "Tell me," she said.

"It's not that I don't think it a lovely image," he said at last. "I'd like as many children as God wills us..."

"But?"

"But I worry for the expense."

Margaret's face fell. Of course.

"I fear my position at the university may only be temporary," he said. "It seems despite being excused of all charges, there are some on the staff still wary of my presence. They fear a stain on the school's reputation."

"You are not responsible for that. It was that horrible

man's doing."

"I know, and I believe they know as well, but I will admit the atmosphere is a bit awkward, if you understand my meaning. One's character, once tainted, isn't always reestablished to its proper place. I fear I have lost respect among my colleagues."

"But you are a hero for saving Peter!"

"But not for losing Ezra."

Margaret's mood fell. Most days she was able to put the horrible events behind her. She no longer looked over her shoulder incessantly as she did at first. She no longer checked the broom closet and cupboards to ensure no one else was in the room. Her comfort had been found in Jonas, in the early days of their wedded bliss and the promise of their future life together. This alone had been enough to get her through the darkest days of the last two months. They had moved from the city, found their cottage, and vowed to have a boring life free of scandal and threat. Slowly but surely the pain of the event released its hold on her and she was able to start anew with a powerful promise of love and hope.

She had never imagined the effect it was having on Jonas's career, however, or the impact to his own mind, and for that she felt ashamed. She had been able to move on. No one in the town knew them or their story save for small snippets in the city newspapers. She found it easy to pretend it never happened, whereas Jonas would have been faced with reminders every day.

"Perhaps we should have gone back to London," she said. She had been happy to stay in Scotland, hoping to give her oldest brother and extended family members enough time to get over the shock of her marrying outside their class. Now she thought this might have been a foolish and somewhat selfish decision.

"I don't think it would have done much good," Jonas confessed. "The news would just find me there as well."

Margaret didn't know what to say. She walked with her head low and her heart lower. "I'm sorry," she said at last, pressing into him in a mimicked hug without slowing their pace.

"Don't be sorry, my darling," he said. "Despite all this, I

remain hopeful I can give you some of the luxuries you have grown accustomed to within the next few years. If you'll just bear with me—"

Margaret forced him to stop. "I don't want luxuries," she said. "I just want you, and our baby." She raised a hand to her belly and smiled. "Whatever you decide, I will be at your side. Forever and for always."

Jonas smiled. "And that, my dear, is why I love you so much." He bent down low and pulled her up into his arms.

"Jonas, no!" she said. "Put me down. Ah!"

The woods echoed with their laughter. The next thirty feet or so of their walk was a playful romp with them both trying to push each other into the snow, hiding behind trees and throwing snowballs. Margaret squealed and Jonas laughed as he finally caught up with her and pulled her back. Together they fell into the snow, out of breath and joyously in love.

A somber look came over Jonas when the sight of Margaret's belly came into view. "Did I hurt you?" he asked, laying a gentle hand over the growing bump.

"I don't think so," she answered. She waited a moment. "I'm fine," she said at last, pulling some snow from beside her and tossing it at him.

"Hey now!"

They scrambled to their feet giggling. Margaret stopped suddenly, her eyes on the path in front of them. A single line of footprints was laid out in the snow, heading where they had just come. "Where did these come from?" she asked.

"I don't know."

Margaret turned in place. Behind them they could clearly see their own path through the snow. Each footfall was crisp and new. The ones in front of them were from a single person.

"They must have come through a while ago," Jonas said. "The snow has already begun to fill them in."

"Were they back there?" she asked, pointing back to Wendall Hall.

"I wasn't paying attention."

Margaret hadn't been paying attention either. "Seems odd, don't you think? We would have seen them. We would have crossed paths. There's no other path from here to Helmsworth. Fannie Mae said so."

"It's probably from hours ago," Jonas said. "The snow isn't so heavy in here. Just someone taking a shortcut to the road."

Margaret nodded. "You're probably right," she said, chuckling at herself. "I'm just being silly."

"Let's keep moving. My toes are nearly frozen. And you'll want to see the street lamps before the snow's too heavy to see anything." Jonas beckoned her toward him and gleefully wrapped his arm around hers. As they walked he pulled her hand up to his mouth and kissed her knuckles. "My love," he said, before he allowed her to place it back in her muff.

Her heart sang at the sensation of it. My love, she thought. What a wonderful feeling.

Chapter 3

Though only twenty miles from Edinburgh, the village of Helmsworth, untouched by the hustle and bustle of the city, sat as shrine to the villages of yesteryear. Its main street boasted a number of shops, including one for draperies and linens, a bakery, a butcher, and a bookstore. A small train depot, which consisted mainly of a platform and small shelter for the ticket master, had been erected at the west end not four years prior. The remaining streets were home to varying houses and cottages, some of its occupants having lived there all their lives while others, Margaret and Jonas included, had been lured by its quiet characteristics and easy access to the commuter train.

Despite its relatively small size, Helmsworth boasted two churches, one which served a denomination of Presbyterians in the region, the other Catholic. Both had been erected opposite each other, flanking the village square, their spires competing in a frozen standoff reaching for the heavens with equal vigour. The competition between the two had been relatively mild, so Margaret was told, until six months ago when one of the Presbyterian elders decided to festoon their spire with an ornate iron cross, an adornment that would at last settle any argument regarding whose was the tallest. This only served to deepen the already simmering feud, however. There was no open animosity, thank goodness, not that Margaret or Jonas could see. Everyone they spoke with seemed happy and welcoming. Any mention of the offending iron cross was done in secret among hushed tones and after many shared pots of tea.

Sadly, the cross did not look long for this world. Margaret could see it from her and Jonas's bedroom window and already it was listing deeply to one side. One good snowstorm and it would be lost for good, Margaret imagined. Such a pity. It was a very nice-looking cross.

That morning started like many others before it. With

much muddling and a few curse words, Margaret threw together something edible for Jonas's breakfast, kept him company while he ate, and saw him off with a kiss at the door. He'd catch the 8:30 train and be at work a few minutes before nine. Margaret would then ready herself with some help from their maid-of-all-work. Annalise came in the morning to clean up breakfast dishes, see that certain parts of the household chores were tended to, and then ready dinner. She'd leave an hour or so before her own husband arrived home from his work in the city.

"You know," she said as she, "many women see to their own households before even thinking of working for some'uh else."

"Yes, I imagine they do, but were I to do that you'd be out the seven shillings I pay you each week."

Annalise was searching for power, Margaret realized. Her words were a reflection of the maid's own insecurities and truly held nothing of value with regard to Margaret's choices as a wife and mother-to-be. Reduced in circumstances, Annalise had been forced into service by the actions of her husband, who spent so much of his own earnings on drink almost as soon as he'd acquired it. Margaret imagined it pained Annalise greatly to leave her own children to do the washing up at another woman's house.

They remained silent until the last pin was placed in Margaret's hair, which was just as well, as Margaret was in no mood for an argument. And she wasn't especially interested in trying to hire someone new so close to the holidays.

"Thank you, Annalise. I can manage from here," Margaret said, lifting her gaze and looking to the maid through the reflection of the mirror. Before the maid left her view Margaret saw her pull a face of annoyance.

Margaret knew her work at Wendall Hall was unconventional but it was the only thing she could think to do while waiting for her own child to arrive. The winter months would be long and lonely were she cooped up in their cottage without a soul to speak to. Margaret never knew an empty house. Growing up there had always been her brothers, friends, visiting family members, and an army of servants just a room or two away. In the city, or even at their country house, she'd have invitations to tea and dances. At this time of year, she'd have Christmas parties nearly every evening and most certainly a ball before Hogmanay. And had she not married Jonas she'd have all these things still.

It was a trade she'd willingly made, but that didn't mean she'd quietly back away to assume the role of doctor's wife and mother. In the previous year, Margaret had grown accustomed to various occupations of her time, many of which were quite unconventional. And Margaret was thankful for the great effect it had had on her. Even though she was in a motherly way she didn't see why she couldn't expand her knowledge further, help those who weren't nearly as fortune, and perhaps explore the possibility of catching babies on her own one day.

Margaret pondered this and more as she made her way down the lane to the main road. Arthur Tillerson and his team of horses waited in the square, only instead of his normal carriage, he had hitched up the sleigh. "Good Morning, Mrs. Davies," he called out at the sight of her. "How do ye like my new bells?" He pulled up the reins slightly, forcing them to jingle. Their chime was nostalgia-inducing, sending waves of Christmas memories tingling up her arms.

"They sound lovely," she said as she approached.

"Where can I take you today?" he asked. He smiled broadly. Their destination never changed and yet every morning he asked as if expecting she'd changed her mind.

"I think Wendall Hall shall do nicely," she said, playing along.

"Very good, ma'am."

Arthur was not her hired driver. In fact, he refused to accept any compensation for his daily efforts to bring her to work. He worked as a delivery man, hired by farmers, shopkeepers, and the like to bring their goods, sold and bought, to the four corners of the county. He'd take items delivered by train from the train depot and disperse them out among the smaller villages and hamlets, those farther from the main rail line and off the well-trodden path. Each day he drove the road from Helmsworth around the outskirts of the city, his route taking him past the old estate of Wendall Hall multiple times each day. It was no trouble, he insisted, and in fact it helped him ready himself with better timing knowing that someone else was waiting for him.

Arthur helped Margaret settle herself on the front bench of his two-bench sleigh and then, reins in hand, he slipped in beside her. "I brought some furs to keep you warm if you'd like," he said, nodding to the blanket between them.

As Margaret laid them over her lap she ran her bare hand over the soft hairs, relishing their luxurious feel and warmth. She did not believe they were entirely necessary, but once the two-horse team began to move and the wind flew at them over the open fields she was thankful they were there.

"Many babies being born these days?" he asked, to pass the time.

"A few," Margaret answered. "I imagine we will be welcoming a few more before Christmas."

He nodded. While some of the locals were divided on the need for such a place as Wendall Hall, most residents having resigned to just forget the place existed at all, others actively supported it and went out of their way to see it succeed. Arthur was one of these supporters.

"Christmas seems a merry time to have a wee one," he said. "The only time I seem to have a hankering for a family of me own is at the holidays. Christmas wasn't much of anything when I were a young'un, but I do like what's been made of it."

Arthur was a confirmed bachelor at fifty. He'd never had time nor need of a wife, he said. He confessed once that if perhaps he'd met Margaret thirty years earlier he'd have changed his mind.

"Are ye looking forward to Christmas, Mrs. Davies?"

"Yes, of course," she said, bristling against the cold wind as they drove the road. "My mother passed away last November so last Christmas was quiet and not at all like the ones my brothers and I had as children," she confessed. "This shall be my first Christmas as a wife."

"And expectant mother," he added, nodding to her torso.

Instinctively, Margaret's hand spread out over her

stomach under her cloak. "If this Christmas be joyful, next year's will be even more so." She smiled as the sleigh rounded the bend and Wendall Hall came into view.

Arthur pulled the horses to a stop at the front gate and offered a hand so Margaret could climb down. "Until tomorrow morning, Mrs. Davies," he said before tipping his hat and heading on down the road.

Margaret made her way through the gate and headed up the snow-covered path. She noticed someone had placed a holly wreath on the front door. It must have been put there that morning as it wasn't dusted with snow like everything else. Instead of using the front door, Margaret circled the building and headed for the side door, the one with a direct path between the building and the barn. She was surprised to find the path even more hindered by snow that had drifted from the roof and the open field behind the building. The door was nearly impassable. She glanced to the barn but saw it was boarded shut against the elements.

Margaret kicked some of the excess snow away with her boot, enough to open the door so she could slide through. When she turned to close it behind her something in the snow caught her eye. She stopped. Leaning in low she saw what appeared to be blood. In a nearby room Margaret heard movement. "Mrs. Gibson, is that you?" she asked, not taking her gaze from the red blotch in the snow.

While standing in the opening of the door, Margaret pulled her hands from her muff and started moving snow to the side with her bare hands.

Seconds later Violet came out into the corridor. "No, Margaret, it's me," she said merrily.

"There's something in the snow," Margaret answered. She'd moved enough snow to open the door wide and she shifted herself outside. It seemed with each movement of her hands, more and more red snow was revealed. Small patches at first and then larger amounts. Then Margaret found something solid. When she wrapped her hand around it she knew instantly what it was and recoiled. She looked back to the door and saw Violet raise a hand to her mouth. "Is that...? Is it...?"

Together they worked furiously, pushing aside patches of snow handfuls at a time from the mound.

"Mrs. Gibson!" Margaret called out, the tone in her voice denoting the panic she felt. "Benson!" It was a body, a frozen body in the snow.

"Margaret, run to the carriage house, fetch Benson!"

Margaret nodded but before she turned to leave the face of the body was revealed through a small opening and she stopped. All the remaining warmth left in her body dropped to her feet at the sight. She fell to her knees.

"Fannie Mae?"

The tears came on quickly, cascading from Margaret's eyes and trailing down her reddened cheeks. "Fannie Mae?" Panicked, she began pulling the snow from her friend's face. Her nostrils were framed with blood and small amounts gathered on the corners of her mouth.

"Is she dead?" Violet asked.

There was no question. Fannie Mae's skin was so cold to the touch. She had no doubt the young woman had been there most of the night. A new round of cries escaped Margaret before she could stop herself.

Not Fannie Mae. Please not her. She was so sweet and caring. She had just had tea with her the evening before. She did not deserve such an end.

"No, no!" Margaret's movements became jagged. She could not feel her hands as she worked to dig her friend out of the snow.

"Margaret."

She fought against Violet's hands, which worked to pull her away.

"Margaret, come please," she said. "There's nothing we can do for her now. Look at your hands." Violet took up Margaret's nearly purple hands. Violet's own hands felt as hot as a poker fresh from the coals compared to Margaret's. "We must warm you up quick."

"No."

"Margaret, think of your baby."

She stopped struggling.

Somehow she managed to stand and walk away from the body. She let Violet guide her to the kitchen where a large fire was already burning. She was set in a chair pulled close to the warmth and was vaguely aware of movement around her.

"Goodness! What's happened?" Mrs. Gibson asked from behind her.

"There's been a..." Violet's voice trailed off. "Summon Benson. I believe he's in the carriage house."

Mrs. Gibson nodded but before she could turn to leave, Violet touched her arm. "And use the front door," she said. "Don't go near the side entrance."

Seconds later Violet was at Margaret's side near the fire. "Put your hands to the fire," Violet instructed, pulling Margaret's damp cloak away from her shoulders. "Margaret?"

Margaret looked up suddenly, aware she was being spoken to.

"Hands toward the fire."

She did as she was told and instantly regretted it. Her hands burned to the point of numbness. The agony was too much and Margaret pulled them away.

"No." Violet forced them back into the warmth.

Margaret gritted her teeth in pain, closed her eyes, and would have slipped from the chair if she thought it would do any good. Her entire body ached from the pain of the cold but her hands, her hands that had been digging to free her dead friend, were burning from the inside out. "Make it stop," she shouted.

"The only way to make it stop is to warm them up," Violet answered. One of the kitchen orderlies entered the room with an armful of blankets. "Thank you," Violet said. "Two for Mrs. Davies and one for me, please."

Margaret felt a blanket being tucked around her lower body and another wrapped around her shoulders, and she was powerless to do anything. It took all her strength of will to keep her hands directed at the warmth. With the addition of the blankets, Margaret noticed the rest of her body slowly warming back up to its normal temperature.

Once the fog of pain loosened its grip on Margaret she was able to organize her thoughts. "When did Fannie Mae leave last night?" she asked. "Was that door locked? Maybe she forgot something and couldn't get back in. How did this happen?"

Violet pulled the blanket higher on her shoulders and stared at something at her feet. "I don't know."

They heard the front door open. Seconds later Benson stumbled in, pushed forward by Mrs. Gibson, who looked fit to box his ears were he not going to do what she commanded. "Found 'im, two sheets to the wind, methinks!"

Benson cringed against the sound of her booming voice. "My apologies, ma'am," Benson said.

Never before had Margaret seen him so sheepish and apologetic. As often the only man among many women he could be quite a curmudgeon.

Violet stood but didn't move far from the warmth of the fire. "What have you been up to, Benson?" she demanded. "I've strictly forbidden the consumption of alcohol on these premises. You know the types of families some of these women have come to us from. No one can feel at ease with drunkenness around them."

"Yes, ma'am. I understand."

"Then tell me, why?" Violet asked. "Why have you broken one of my carnal rules?"

"Someone left me a bottle of gin in the carriage house. It were tied with a bow an' everything. I thought it were an early Christmas present from yerself, ma'am."

"I'd never gift such a horrendous substance," she said, her expression further emphasizing her distaste.

Benson looked more than a little uncomfortable with so much attention placed on him. He avoided Margaret's gaze completely and Violet's as well.

"Fannie Mae wasn't imbibing in the barn with you, was she?" Mrs. Gibson asked, chuckling slightly. "I have to tell you, Ms. Violet, I haven't seen her all morning."

Margaret felt sadness rising again from the pit of her stomach at the mention of Fannie Mae. Violet must have seen this too. She took two steps to Margaret and rested a hand on her shoulder in comfort.

Mrs. Gibson noticed none of this and continued in the same jocular manner. "Lord knows what sort of trouble that girl has gotten herself into."

The three women and a swaying Benson, still affected by

too much drink, went out to the side door.

"Heavens have mercy," Mrs. Gibson said, crossing herself.

"Benson, are you well enough to drive the carriage?" Violet asked, her face stoic and somewhat stern. "You must go to Haddington and inform the police."

With a doubtful look, Benson nodded. "I'll go with him. Can't have him driving off into a stream given his condition," Mrs. Gibson said. "As long as you can have one of the other girls see to the wee ones, including my boy."

"Yes, of course. Go then, quick as you can," Violet said.

The pair scurried off, leaving Margaret and Violet standing over the body.

"We should bring her inside," Violet said, kneeling down to move the body.

"No, we mustn't move her," Margaret said, grabbing Violet's arm to stop her from touching anything.

Violet paused and looked up. "We can't just leave her here."

"I'm afraid we must. The police will want to investigate the scene. She mustn't be moved until the investigation concludes," Margaret explained.

Margaret would admit it seemed cruel to leave someone they cared about in such a state but she could see no other way. Before heading inside, Margaret removed the blanket that was around her shoulders and laid it over Fannie Mae's blue-tinged face and the snowy mound that hid the rest of her frozen body. With a hand resting on top of the blanket, Margaret remained crouching for a moment, unable to move away. She bowed her head and began to cry again.

Violet pulled her up from the ground and brought her back into the building.

"What's all this?" asked a familiar voice down the hall.

Margaret and Violet looked up. Standing outside the door to the cloakroom, pink in the cheeks and very much alive, was Fannie Mae.

Chapter 4

Margaret could scarcely move. She stood as still as a statue, allowing the seconds to pass before she looked to Violet. Yes, the head matron saw Fannie Mae as well. Margaret was not losing her mind. Simultaneously, both women began crying. Fannie Mae came toward them, laughing and bewildered. "What's the matter? My goodness... what...?"

Margaret touched Fannie Mae's arm first, to ensure she was alive, before wrapping her arms around her and squeezing tightly. Behind her, Margaret felt Violet join the embrace as well, though her enthusiasm was far more subdued.

"I don't think I have ever been welcomed to work as warmly as this," Fannie Mae said from the centre of the circle.

"We thought you were dead," Margaret said as she pulled away. She didn't release her grip on Fannie Mae's hands.

"Oh, Margaret, your hands are so cold." Fannie Mae wrapped both her hands around Margaret's and raised them to her mouth to blow on them. She rubbed her hands over Margaret's to help circulate the blood. "I'm not dead."

"No, no you're not. Thank the heavens." Margaret was so happy she cared little for the pain in her hands. Seconds passed in relief and jubilation before her eyes went wide. "If you're not dead"—she looked to the door behind them and then looked to Violet—"then who's out there?"

ès ∽

Margaret watched Fannie Mae closely as they stood next to the blanket. She held her hands in her own tightly as Violet poised herself over the head of the body, still covered by the blanket Margaret had placed there.

"This will alarm you," Margaret warned. "Brace yourself."

She felt Fannie Mae's body stiffen. When she was ready,

she nodded toward Violet.

Fannie Mae gasped at the sight. She pulled her hands from Margaret's and covered her face as she turned away. "I feel ill," Margaret heard her say as Fannie Mae paced to the gate and back again. She stopped a few feet from Margaret but wasn't able to look at her. Margaret's own heart raced at the sight of the body—only now her friend Fannie Mae stood before her, alive and well, while an exact copy, a twin, lay dead on the walkway.

"I don't understand," Fannie Mae said at last, placing a hand over her stomach. "Who is this woman? How did she get here? And why does she look like me?"

"I share those questions," Margaret said, closing the gap between them. "I'm afraid we don't have any answers for you."

"We've sent for the police," Violet said.

Margaret looked over her shoulder at Violet, who appeared sullen and meek in the dim morning light. There had been something in her voice too, a quiver of fear that she was trying to mask with her usual air of authority. Margaret wondered if this was how she coped with most things.

"I don't understand..." Fannie Mae's words became jumbled, bursting forth in fits and starts but never forming complete sentences. After a few tries she gave up and used both her hands to hide her face.

"Your confusion is warranted," Margaret said. "We are all confused."

"I haven't the faintest idea who this woman could be," Fannie Mae said.

"Whoever she is, she's someone's daughter at least. We have to find out who she is and notify her family. Maybe we will be able to discover why she was here," Margaret said.

Fannie Mae nodded as she hugged her body against the cold.

"Perhaps we should just leave it to the police," Violet suggested.

"I have to find out who she is," Fannie Mae said. "She could be a relative of some kind... well, I mean, she has to be, doesn't she? It's more than just coincidence, right?"

Margaret nodded. "I certainly think so," she said.

"I won't be able to rest until I know." Fannie Mae was looking to them and seeking agreement. At the very least she wanted to know she could count on them for support, or so Margaret thought. Violet appeared hesitant but Margaret was already emotionally invested. Just like all the others, she needed to see this through. She needed to solve the mystery and give a grieving family the answers they desperately needed.

"I want to know who did this to her," Margaret said, mirroring Fannie Mae's determination. "And I want to know why."

Fannie Mae allowed a small smile to creep up the sides of her mouth. "That's the spirit," Fannie Mae said. "I knew you were a kindred spirit the moment I clamped eyes on you."

An hour passed before Mrs. Gibson and Benson returned with an officer from Haddington close at their heels. Margaret could tell they had been rushing by their manner of speaking, out of breath and apologetic. "We went as quick as we could," Benson said.

Mrs. Gibson nodded behind him. "He comes," she said, "not a minute behind."

In that instant, a slight but commanding young man entered the room. A stockier fellow in a matching navy blue uniform lurked in the corridor behind him.

"Deputy Chief Constable Andrew Kelly, at your service, ma'am," he said, with a hand placed formally over his heart. Margaret wasn't sure if the ma'am he spoke of was her or Violet or someone else entirely as he looked none of them in the eye. "Where is the body?"

Margaret watched from the hall as Violet took them outside. Thankfully, they left the door open so both Margaret and Fannie Mae could hear what was said, though they both pretended as though they were not paying particular attention.

The heavier-set man bent low to the ground while Chief Deputy Kelly stood. Margaret watched out the corner of her eye as both men took in the sight of the body and looked down the hall at Fannie Mae. In the seconds that passed, confusion took hold.

"Is this woman known to you?" Chief Deputy Kelly asked. His eyes darted to Fannie Mae, perhaps expecting her to answer with an affirmation.

"We don't know this woman at all," Violet explained. "At first, we thought it was Fannie Mae, one of our nurses, but as you can see she is quite well."

Margaret felt Fannie Mae shift uncomfortably at her side. "Feels quite disconcerting to suddenly have a twin," she said, quietly so only Margaret could hear, "even more so to see her dead."

"I don't doubt it," Margaret answered.

They watched as the two policemen poked the dead woman's cheek, as if ensuring it were real.

"What do they expect?" Mrs. Gibson asked, coming out the doorway of the nursery and watching the policemen alongside Margaret. "Yes, we've created a dummy to look and feel real and staged a murder for our own merriment."

Fannie Mae released a snort of laughter, a noise that brought barbed attention from Violet. Chagrined, Fannie Mae placed a hand over her mouth as if to prevent a further outburst.

"Both these men are acting as if it's some sort of charade," Mrs. Gibson continued, keeping her volume low. "I mean, would it do any harm to simply believe people every once in a while?"

Margaret had had her share of interactions with policemen, both in London and Edinburgh, and it seemed abject suspicion was the gold standard for investigators. She looked forward to the day when a police officer took her at her word and properly pursued the criminal instead of wasting valuable time by subjecting her and the ones she loved to ruthless accusations.

"My brother could determine her cause of death within the hour," Margaret said. "Give him a few days and he'd probably be able to track down the culprits too."

"Your brother, the doctor?" Fannie Mae asked.

"He's a surgeon, actually."

"Why don't you send for him?"

Margaret shook her head. "No. It's far too long a journey. And he has his fiancée and adopted little girl to think of."

"What about your husband? Can he do what your brother does?" Mrs. Gibson asked.

Margaret was sure he could and had every intention of involving him in their plight for the truth. But she also didn't want to worry him, not after everything that happened in Edinburgh. They had been hoping their move to Helmsworth would give them a nice, quiet routine with which to relax while they waited for their firstborn to arrive. Now it seemed death and calamity had followed them east. Somehow she must get word to him that she was all right.

"Mrs. Davies?"

Margaret looked up to find both policemen and Violet were looking at her through the open doorway.

"May we have a word with you?" Kelly asked.

"Of course." Margaret met them at the door.

"Do you mind showing me your path as you came to work this morning?" Kelly asked, stepping back so she could indicate where she walked.

"I get dropped at the front road—"

"Who drops you off?" Kelly interjected.

"Arthur Tillerson. He gives me a ride every morning from the village square in Helmsworth."

Violet shifted uncomfortably and looked to the officer as if to ask if such an arrangement were permissible. It was clear she hadn't realized until then how Margaret had made herself so punctual.

"Where did you go after you were deposited by Mr. Tillerson?"

"I came up the front walkway."

"And you didn't use the front door?" He seemed to think Margaret should have done so.

"No, I didn't," Margaret answered. "I didn't wish to disturb our guests."

The second officer gave a smile. "Is this a hotel then?" he asked.

Margaret's gaze shot to Violet, who stood a few feet away. The look on Violet's face was conciliatory but not altogether helpful.

"It does not matter why I did or didn't use the front door," Margaret said forcibly. "All that matters is that I didn't. I used the side door, as I always do. There was a drift of snow in front of it and I had to move quite a bit aside with my boot to get to the door. I only saw some drops of blood when I turned to close the door behind me."

"Drops of blood where?" Kelly asked.

Margaret looked down but found the snow in the immediate area around the body had been compressed and changed by the number of people who had visited the scene. "I don't see them now," she said. "It must be all the foot traffic. We've contaminated the scene."

"What did you just say?" Kelly moved close as if he were hard of hearing.

"We've contaminated the scene," Margaret repeated. "It looks different than when I first found her."

"And whose fault is that?"

"I tried to help someone in distress."

"The woman's dead, how much help can you administer?"

"I didn't know she was dead at the time." Margaret was getting angry now. She felt blood rising to her cheek as her heart quickened.

Kelly positioned his pencil inside his palm-sized notebook and lowered it in front of him. "Thank you, Mrs. Davies. That will be all for now."

Reluctantly, Margaret returned to the warmth of the building. Like many of her interviews with police, she felt there was more she could add to the investigation, like how she had thought she saw something near the carriage house the night before or that they should shovel much of the snow from the yard to search for the weapon. In the end, she remained quiet and walked back to Fannie Mae.

"That looked delightful," Fannie Mae said quietly.

"Hardly."

"Miss Harris?"

Fannie Mae looked to the end of the hall. Kelly had left his constable and Benson outside to shovel out the body and was now standing near a closed door. "A word, if I may." He gestured to a nearby internal door.

"Is Margaret permitted as well?" Fannie Mae asked.

Kelly looked displeased at the suggestion but by law he had to oblige. "Of course."

Chapter 5

Deputy Chief Kelly led Margaret and Fannie Mae into Violet's office on the main floor. He pulled one of the chairs intended for clients back from the desk and indicated for Fannie Mae to sit down. "We'll start once you get comfortable," he said, his voice denoting a certain degree of disinterest.

Margaret chose to stand and held back at the door.

He took the chair behind the desk, positioning himself as the authority in the room and behaving as if they had all just come to see him. Margaret saw him scan the desktop papers. He'd not find anything of interest, Margaret assured herself. Violet was quite neat and orderly. She'd never have offered the space if she thought Kelly would become privy to client information.

"Who is that woman to you?" he asked, notebook at the ready.

"I've never seen that woman before in my life," Fannie Mae said.

"But you do see the resemblance?"

"Yes, of course. How could one not?" Fannie Mae's voice was weak and quiet. She was still in a fair bit of shock, Margaret was certain.

Kelly regarded her suspiciously, as if trying to decide if she spoke in earnest. Officers of the law all seemed to have such a look. It must have been taught to them as part of their initial training. It was a cross between curiosity and detachment. Margaret knew the look well.

"Tell me about your situation," he said. When Fannie Mae didn't immediately answer, he elaborated. "Are you married?"

"No, sir."

"Do you live at home with your parents? Do you have any siblings?"

"I live with my mother. My father has passed on. I have no siblings."

"Any cousins? Aunts? Uncles?"

Fannie Mae shook her head. "My mother's sister lives near Glasgow. She never married."

"And your father's people?"

She looked genuinely uneasy. "I don't see how this pertains to the dead woman."

"I assure you, it does." Kelly had not written a single thing in his book. He merely looked on, unaffected by the manner in which his questions made Fannie Mae uncomfortable. "Answer the question."

Fannie Mae swallowed. "My father was a foundling, sir. He has never had any family of his own." She looked back to Margaret apologetically as the graphite scratched away on Kelly's notebook. Margaret did not know much about Fannie Mae's family. She knew Fannie Mae's father had died. The women had bonded on the fact since Margaret had lost both her parents in the previous year. Margaret had not been aware that Mr. Harris had been a foundling. Perhaps it had been a family secret, something which Fannie Mae had never intended for Margaret to know. It could also have been something that just never came up in conversation.

"And where do you and your mother live?"

"In Helmsworth, but not quite. We have a cottage near Montley Road."

"I'll have to speak with her," he said, raising his eyes. "Your mother."

Fannie Mae nodded. "Of course." She released a breath, a reminder to Margaret, who had been inadvertently holding her own.

"Can you account for your whereabouts this morning?"

"I awoke at five, or thereabouts. Every morning I help my mother with breakfast for our boarders. We have three at present. An older gentleman who's only in the area a short time and—"

"Never mind that. What did you do after breakfast?"

It took a moment for Fannie Mae to recover from Kelly's rebuke. She fumbled with her words and then rubbed her open palms on her skirt. "Well... I...I left the house nearer to seven and came here."

"How did you travel?"

"Annabelle...er... my horse. She's in the carriage house."

"And last night?"

"Yes, I rode my horse last night. My mother and I haven't a carriage—"

"I meant, your whereabouts last evening."

"Right...yes, of course." Fannie Mae closed her eyes, embarrassed about her confusion. "I helped my mother serve dinner, then we wrapped some parcels for the post. I received word that a patient was in labour and Mrs. Davies was all alone, so I came straight back here. Mrs. Bane had been away in Edinburgh for the day." Fannie Mae flashed a tiny smile in Margaret's direction.

"When did you arrive here?"

"I left the house at eight, so I imagine I arrived at nearly eight thirty."

Kelly glanced to Margaret, who was quick to nod. "That sounds about right, yes."

"And when did you leave?"

"I helped Violet make the final rounds around nine thirty. It must have been after ten when I finally left."

"Which door did you leave by?"

"The front door. Violet asked me to hang the wreath. I did so and went straight to the barn."

Deputy Chief Kelly pursed his lips as he pondered this. "Mrs. Bane, she lives on the premises, yes?"

"Yes, sir. She has her own suite of rooms in the adjoining wing. She doesn't want to be too far should anything happen to one of the women."

"Who checks on the women in the night?" he asked.

"Mrs. Gibson, the nursery maid, or one of the other girls. I know last night Mrs. Gibson was on duty for the newborns, and she will sometimes go about to make sure no one is in need of anything."

"The nursery is very handy to that side door." Kelly was not asking, merely stating, as if speaking out loud and not in need of an affirmative response. Fannie Mae did not realize this.

"Yes. I'm sure if she had seen anything or heard anything she'd have said something. She's not the sort to cower, is she, Margaret?"

"No, sir," Margaret said. "She has a very direct manner."

Kelly scratched away with his pencil. "And you, Mrs. Davies... When did you leave?"

Margaret started at the direct question. Her mind had wandered to the image of the dead woman, something she knew would never entirely leave her.

"When did you leave?" he repeated, enunciating each word as if she were new to the English language. She chose to ignore his manner of addressing her.

"My husband came to see me home shortly after Fannie Mae arrived. It was just after nine when we left. We took the route through the woods."

Kelly paused his pencil. "You would have used the side door."

"Yes, sir," Margaret answered.

"And you, nor your husband, saw anything at that time?"

"No. If anyone had been lying there we would have seen it. Most of the snow had accumulated overnight."

Kelly nodded and for the first time his expression changed from suspicion to disappointment.

"We did see something in the woods," Margaret said, suddenly remembering their walk home. "We were walking toward Helmsworth and we saw a set of footprints heading toward Wendall Hall. We found it somewhat odd as we hadn't passed anyone in the woods and no one had arrived at the Hall that evening, other than Fannie Mae and my husband."

"It is quite a distance to town from here," Fannie Mae chimed in.

"And yet Mrs. Davies attempted it in her current condition," Kelly noted.

"Only because we had no alternative," Margaret said. "Besides, exercise is good for the child, or so my husband tells me." Absently Margaret raised a hand to her stomach.

"He's a doctor," Fannie Mae said quickly.

Kelly raised an eyebrow.

"He works with the University of Edinburgh," Margaret said. "Research, mostly."

"And does he teach?"

Margaret didn't bother to hide her feelings on the matter. "Not anymore."

"Why not?"

This question startled Margaret. She couldn't very well confess it was because the university and student body disfavored him. Nor could she say exactly why he had fallen out of favour. He had been a celebrated physician once, revered for his intellect, keen observations, and approachable manner, a remnant of his humble upbringing. Unfortunately, his high standing and prospects of advancements had been crippled by false accusations of murder, something Jonas was nearly certain he'd never recover from. Margaret couldn't say any of this to the officer, though. It would only muddy the already murky waters and cast suspicion where there should be none. Neither Jonas nor Margaret had anything to do with this woman's death. Besides, how was any of this pertinent to Deputy Chief Kelly's current investigation?

"Disagreements with other members of the staff," she said, without missing a beat.

The room fell silent for a moment as Kelly reviewed his notes.

"Miss Harris, you said you don't know this woman," he said.

"That's right."

"Could she be a distant relative of some kind, one of your father's unknown kin who bears a striking resemblance?"

Fannie Mae shrugged. "I suppose anything is possible."

Kelly regarded her expectantly.

"I don't know anything about it," she confessed. "He never spoke about it with me. I wouldn't even know where to tell you to start."

"Perhaps I will start with your mother then."

"My mother?" Fannie Mae seemed genuinely concerned at the prospect. She looked to Margaret. "Perhaps she's already heard about my death. You know how news travels these roads faster than any carriage."

Margaret shared her concern. "We will go to her and show her you are unharmed," Margaret answered. "And hope she hasn't heard anything yet."

Fannie Mae was only somewhat appeased by Margaret's reassurance.

"You may inform your mother of my intention to speak with her. I'd like to know if this woman is some distant relative and not some joke played at my expense," Kelly said, without lifting his gaze from his notebook. "That is all, ladies." He looked up. "You may leave."

Margaret waited for Fannie Mae to meet her at the door. Together they walked into the hall. Fannie Mae released a heavy breath and placed a hand over her stomach. "Are all police interviews so gut wrenching?" she asked.

"I'm afraid so," Margaret replied. "Until they get the answers they need, everyone is suspect. It is the nature of inquiry."

Chapter 6

After gently rapping at the door, Margaret entered Room 205 to find Maisie out of bed and standing near the window overlooking the carriage house and side garden.

"You're up," Margaret said with a smile. "That's a good sign." She entered the room, surveying it for hints regarding anything Maisie might need. "Do you have enough blankets?" she asked, moving to the side of the bed to adjust Maisie's pillows. "I don't want you to be cold."

"Yes. I'm fine." Maisie didn't take her eyes from the landscape beyond the window. "What's going on out there?" She finally turned her head to look at Margaret. "So many people. I don't think I've seen as much movement since I came here."

Margaret blanched. She had come up to the second floor, assured that making the rounds and checking a few patients would take her mind from the awful events of that morning. She debated whether to tell Maisie or not and wondered if Violet would want her to. "I can't rightly say."

"You can't say or you don't want to say?" Maisie smiled. "I may be young, Mrs. Davies, but I ain't stupid."

"I never said you were." Margaret crossed the room and met Maisie at the window. Together they looked out over the snow-covered garden. Chief Deputy Kelly's constable and Benson were shoveling trenches of snow around the area where the body had been found while Kelly stood back observing, every once in a while kicking some snow with his boot.

The view from Maisie's window didn't reveal the exact area of the body. The overhang above the side door obscured the view and prevented Maisie from seeing all Margaret had seen that morning.

"I saw them carrying someone out on a stretcher," Maisie said, her tone soft and melancholy. "A woman died, didn't she?"

Margaret closed her eyes, still unsure how much Violet

would wish her to reveal.

Seeing the look on Margaret's face must have confirmed her suspicions enough. Maisie started to weep, sweeping tears from her lower eyelids and choking back the sadness.

"T'isn't fair, Mrs. Davies. She may have been an unwed mother like me but she deserved to bring her child forth into the world, to see it bring joy to another family. She didn't deserve to die. Was it the fever? Or perhaps the pain was too much."

Margaret stammered. "Maisie..."

"Oh no." Maisie's face blanched and a new, more energetic round of tears began. "The child didn't make it either? Say it isn't so. The poor wee thing."

"No, Maisie, the woman wasn't a patient, well, not that we know of. She didn't die in her child bed."

Maisie tore her eyes from Margaret and looked beyond the glass again, a look of confusion spreading over her features. "But... I thought..."

"No..." Margaret raised a hand to her mouth, unsure how to say it. "When I arrived this morning I found a woman's body in the snow. We believe she died sometime in the night. She didn't die in childbirth." She decided she wouldn't say anything about the woman resembling Fannie Mae.

As Margaret spoke, Maisie's gaze trailed the side garden. She was quiet for a few moments after Margaret finished. "This was last night?" she asked.

Margaret nodded.

"I think I saw something near the carriage house. A man, I think. Keeping to the shadows."

Maisie closed her eyes as if trying to recall her memory with better clarity. She shook her head, uncertain. "I thought it was a trick of the snow at first but I kept my eye on him. He was there."

"Why didn't you say anything?" Margaret asked.

"Everyone was asleep, or would be soon. I didn't wish to be a bother."

Margaret tried not to show her concern. Men were not allowed in the building, save for Benson, Jonas, and a few others who'd never be permitted on the upper floors, not unless they were a doctor specifically asked to assist with a birth. Violet had hinted at a scary situation during Wendall Hall's first year when the father of a patient arrived unexpectedly. He broke into her room and would have done terrible damage to her had Benson not intervened. Since then, Violet had enacted very strict rules with the safety of the patients in mind. "Some of the women come from dubious backgrounds, and have only come here for the sake of their babies," Violet had explained when Margaret first took her position. "It's difficult not to think of what awaits some women when they leave here. I do my best for the children and in a way feel like I am helping the women also."

A man seen lurking outside at night would definitely be considered suspicious, even if a woman hadn't just been murdered.

Margaret eyed the carriage house. "When was this?"

"Last evening, after Mrs. Bane left me for the night. I couldn't sleep and I didn't dare walk. I lay in bed looking out the window to keep my mind off…"

"Christina." Margaret's words were not a question.

Maisie nodded.

Margaret turned and headed back toward the bed. "May I?" she asked, gesturing with her hand toward where Maisie would have been lying. Maisie squared her shoulders to Margaret, hugging herself, and gave a permissive nod.

Gingerly Margaret hoisted herself into the bed, raising her legs up over the edge, and lay back into the pillows. As if understanding Margaret's intention, Maisie stepped back from the window to allow her an unobstructed view.

From the bed Margaret could see a small portion of the trodden path leading from the side door. She could see the low gate at the stone wall and the carriage house beyond. She had a clear view of the front carriage house doors, the lanterns on both sides, and the path Margaret and Jonas had taken to reach the backwoods.

A knock sounded at the door. Acting on impulse, Margaret forced her legs around the side of the bed and stood at attention as the door opened. "Margaret?" Violet Bane peered around the edge of the door before stepping into the room.

"Yes." Slowly Margaret circled the bed. "Fannie Mae has

sent me to fetch you. She said you had offered to go with her to speak with her mother about"—her eyes went to Maisie—"about what happened today."

"Yes, of course. She is ready then?"

Violet nodded and gave a small smile.

"Tell her I shall be down presently."

Violet looked to Maisie then, as the girl shuffled back toward her bed. "Are you resting, Maisie? We don't want to hinder your recovery. I need you on the mend before we think of sending you back to your employer."

"Yes, ma'am."

Margaret helped Maisie return to her bed, positioning her pillows so she could sit up somewhat and then bringing the blankets up to her waist. "I shall check on you again once I return," Margaret said, laying a soft hand over Maisie's on the blanket. "Make sure to eat something, even if you don't feel like it."

Maisie gave a small nod. Margaret could tell she was tired and ready for another nap. They'd have to watch her closely over the next day to ensure there was no fever or melancholy. Birth mothers who were forced to give up their children were at greater risk of hysteria and other maladies. Margaret certainly didn't want Maisie to fall victim to either.

In the hall Violet waited while Margaret closed the door softly behind her.

"How is Fannie Mae?" she asked quietly, as soon as they were alone.

Margaret opened her mouth to speak but couldn't find the right words. She wondered if Fannie Mae would want Margaret to speak of her to Violet, their employer. In many respects the relationships between the staff at Wendall Hall was amicable. They all liked each other and worked together well. Aside from Benson, one of the only men about the building, the staff of ten was mostly women with a common understanding of the needs of women, rich or poor, who find themselves in dire need. But it was clear Violet, although approachable and fair, had made a point to keep herself separate from her charges. Fannie Mae had told Margaret once that Violet viewed herself as mother superior to all who darkened the doors. She gave orders and expected them to be acted upon. She was so exacting no one ever challenged her authority, which overall contributed to the well-established management of the charity. Violet had allowed a wall to be positioned between her and her staff. Margaret observed the stunted unease between Violet and the others, something that didn't seem to exist between Violet and Margaret.

Margaret wondered if perhaps it was because the women were from a similar class. As much as Margaret wished to be respected as a doctor's wife, and doctor's wife only, she was aware that the manner of her speech, the vocabulary she inherently chose, and the aesthetic of her dress were all very indicative of her high-class upbringing. Perhaps Violet, despite her desire to help all classes and despite having done so for a number of years, still allowed societal division to dictate her view of others. While Margaret wanted to believe she and Violet got on because of some personal connection she could not help but think it was more rooted in something beyond Margaret's and even Fannie Mae's personal control.

Violet hesitated at the top of the stairs, turning toward Margaret and expecting her to pause as well. "I would ask her myself except I know you are far more connected with her. Has she recovered from the shock?" Violet's hand came out and rested on Margaret's arm. "Have you, my dear?"

"I think you are right to be concerned for Fannie Mae. She is still very perplexed as to how someone can look so much like her."

Violet nodded. Her eyes were trained on Margaret, but she could tell her mind wandered elsewhere.

"I think she may just need some time," Margaret added. "And I believe she is anxious to speak with her mother before the rumours make their rounds."

Suddenly, Violet's attention returned and she released Margaret's arm. "Oh, yes, of course. She must go to her mother." A tiny smile escaped the matron. "You both should take your time. I can handle everything here in your absence."

Margaret started down the stairs, aware that Violet chose not to follow her. At the turn Margaret glanced up and saw Violet still in the same spot, her eyes focused on something on the floor. She looked sad, almost lost. Margaret wondered if all their attention should be directed toward Fannie Mae. Perhaps they should also be keeping a close eye on Violet Bane.

☙ ❧

Benson drove both women, Margaret and Fannie Mae, to Helmsworth in the estate carriage, taking his time over the snow-covered roads. He said little during the journey despite opening his mouth and turning his face toward them as if he meant to. Margaret and Fannie Mae kept their conversation subdued, speaking only of the snow, the cold, and the coming holidays. At many times they allowed themselves to fall silent, watching the passing landscape instead, huddling against the cold, and taking in the various decorations adorning the houses as they passed.

By the time they reached the village, the odd wreath or red bow in the country turned into an all-encompassing display of the Christmas season. Bows and wreaths were festooned to each street lantern. Garland could be seen on every length of fence with beautifully large bows at each gathering point. A sleigh passed them on the road, jingling its bells as the horses trotted along.

Margaret turned to Fannie Mae. "Is Helmsworth always so festive during the holidays?"

"Oh yes," Fannie Mae said. "Mother says it's on account of the churches. Neither of them wishes to be outdone by the other. The parishioners are a competitive bunch. Once trees and greenery were adopted as tradition there seemed to be no stopping them."

"Why should anyone wish to stop them?" Margaret asked. "Helmsworth must be the prettiest little town I have ever seen."

"You aren't the only one to say so," Fannie Mae said. "After Father died, Mother's sister asked if she'd be better to return to Glasgow. Mother wouldn't hear of it. And I am truly glad for it. Imagine growing up in the city and missing all of this. Such a dirty, stinky place. Made even worse now with all the factories and such." Fannie Mae smiled. "Glasgow is certainly nice to visit, but Helmsworth is my home and I do believe it always shall be."

Margaret smiled at the notion. She wished she could say the same. In no other time of her life had she been so happy. But her future with Jonas was less certain. His job with the university might only be temporary. Before long they might need to uproot once more. She did not say any of this to Fannie Mae, of course. She was smiling giddily as they made their way through town, the first smile Margaret had seen on her since that morning. Margaret had no interest in taking it away.

Benson pulled the carriage to a stop in front of Fannie Mae's front gate. Achingly, he turned to help the women alight but realized quickly neither needed his assistance.

"Thank you, Benson," Margaret and Fannie Mae said in near unison.

"Mrs. Bane has sent me for a few items at the shops. When you have a mind to return to the Hall ye shall find me there," he said, his gruff manner from the night before a thing of the past.

Margaret and Fannie Mae nodded.

He waved to them and shuffled back to his seat.

"Well now, someone has certainly changed his tune since yesterday," Fannie Mae said to Margaret as the carriage pulled away.

"I do believe he was genuinely grief-stricken when he heard of your passing," Margaret said, realizing she had dropped her muff in the snow at her feet. "He may act like a cantankerous old goat but that may not be the truth of it," she said and she bent down to grab it.

When she looked to Fannie Mae, muff in her hand, she found her friend staring solemnly at the front door. "Fannie Mae?"

"What if she's heard something?" Fannie Mae looked to Margaret, her face panic-stricken at the thought of her mother grieving the death of her daughter without cause. "What if she's beside herself with grief? I could not live with myself. She does not deserve such tragedy."

Margaret spied tears in Fannie Mae's eyes.

"We mustn't delay," Margaret answered, taking a step forward and coaxing Fannie Mae to follow. "If she is grief-stricken we are best to explain it all as quickly as possible."

Fannie Mae nodded and finally followed Margaret's lead.

At the door Fannie Mae pushed her way inside, and ushered Margaret in after her. Once inside they closed the door, thankful for the warmth, and stood to listen. Gentle sobbing could be heard from one of the rooms at the back of the house. Without bothering to take off her outer clothes, Fannie Mae hurried toward the sound.

"Mama?"

Margaret followed along after her, walking the length of a central hall before finally reaching a larger opening, the kitchen, where Mrs. Harris sat crying into her hands while another woman stood at her side rubbing her shoulders.

"Mama!" Fannie Mae took another step forward. "I'm all right," she said, removing her fur-trimmed hat.

Mrs. Harris looked up slowly, revealing bloodshot eyes and ruddy, tear-stained cheeks. She stood suddenly at the sight of her daughter. Shocked and bewildered, Margaret watched as the woman's lower lip quivered at the sight.

Fannie Mae stepped forward, opening her arms for an embrace. But before she could reach her mother, Mrs. Harris collapsed on the floor.

Chapter 8

Fannie Mae rushed to her mother's side while the woman who had been consoling her dropped into a kitchen chair behind her.

"Mama! Mama!" Fannie Mae gave her mother light taps on her cheek in the hopes it would bring her around.

Quickly Margaret pulled a glass from beside the sink and filled it with water. By the time she turned to Fannie Mae, Mrs. Harris was coming around. Her head moved as if still in a dream, her lips releasing slight murmurs before her eyes opened. Holding her mother's cheek in her hand, Fannie Mae smiled. "I am not dead, Mama," she said softly. "It was all a misunderstanding."

Margaret went to her knees beside them, as quickly as her round belly would allow, and held the glass of water in anticipation. Fannie Mae used the water to wet her fingers and then pressed them onto her mother's forehead and cheeks.

"Oh lord, have mercy," the woman seated at the table said. She hid her face with her hands, sneaking peaks at Fannie Mae and Margaret on the ground as if not believing it.

"Margaret, this is our neighbour, Mrs. Isabella Price," Fannie Mae said, gesturing with a nod of her head.

Mrs. Harris moved her hand, reaching up to her daughter's face. Fannie Mae smiled and then wrapped her own hand into her mother's grasp. "I am real, Mama," she said.

"Isabella said you were dead," Mrs. Harris said, her words coming slowly, still unsure.

"It is not Mrs. Price's fault." Fannie Mae glanced to Margaret. "There was a mistake. I am all right. See?" Fannie Mae took her mother's hands and placed it on the side of her cheek. Mrs. Harris's eyes closed and she wept openly.

It took some time before Fannie Mae and Margaret were able to get Mrs. Harris from the ground and into a soft chair in the sitting room. Mrs. Price had agreed to make them all tea, shaking her head in disbelief before leaving the room, while Margaret and Fannie Mae peeled off their layers of warm clothing.

"Everyone in the village is talking about it," Mrs. Price said, returning to the room as Margaret settled into one of the upholstered chairs. Fannie Mae knelt in front of her mother, taking the older woman's hands in her own.

"Mama, this is my friend, Margaret Davies, the woman I talked to you about from London," Fannie Mae said, gesturing to Margaret. "Her husband is the doctor."

Mrs. Harris nodded and smiled in Margaret's direction but said nothing, still reeling from her earlier shock.

"Dr. and Mrs. Davies who have moved into Churchill Cottage?" Mrs. Price asked, standing over Margaret, a teacup and saucer in her hand.

"That's right," Margaret said. "We've lived there nearly six weeks."

"Your servant, Annalise, you should dismiss her," Mrs. Price said.

"Whatever for?"

"Her husband has been talking about ye to all who will listen, the drunkard." Mrs. Price scrunched up her nose and shook her head in disbelief. "Everyone knows you ain't much of a cook and that your husband dons an apron to help ye with the cleanin'."

"He does not wear an apron. What a horrid thing to say!"

Mrs. Price raised an eyebrow. "So he does help with the women's work, then?"

Margaret feigned nonchalance. "Why shouldn't he?"

The look Mrs. Price gave Margaret radiated her amusement. She handed Margaret the teacup and saucer with all the grace of a ten-year-old who imagined they had better things to do.

"Well, I'm not about to punish a woman because of the actions of her husband," Margaret said, as Mrs. Price returned to the tea tray. She looked to Fannie Mae and found her friend and her mother had not witnessed the exchange. Fannie Mae looked to her mother apologetically, pressing her cheek into her mother's open hand. A few tears still lingered on Mrs. Harris's cheeks.

"Margaret and I can explain everything," Fannie Mae said, "Though some of it may be rather difficult to hear."

"Whatever you tell me, it won't be near as difficult as hearing my precious daughter has passed. Honestly, Fannie Mae, I've lost your father. I simply cannot bear to lose you as well."

Mrs. Harris's words made Fannie Mae smile. "Someone has died, Mama," she said. "But it wasn't me... only..." She looked to Margaret imploringly, unsure how to explain the events of that morning.

Margaret put down her tea and inched to the edge of her seat. "Mrs. Harris, when I arrived at Wendall Hall this morning I stumbled upon someone just outside the side door," she began. "This person had passed away sometime in the night and had been covered with a great deal of snow. I mistakenly believed it was Fannie Mae."

A slight chuckle escaped Mrs. Harris before the woman squeezed her daughter's hand tighter. "I am sorry for the girl, but I am deeply glad it was not my girl."

"It seems a rather odd conclusion, Mrs. Davies, to mistake one dead girl for another," Mrs. Price said taking a seat at the opposite end of the sofa from Mrs. Harris.

"It wasn't Margaret's fault," Fannie Mae said quickly. "The woman... well, she looks just like me, in every way." She looked to Margaret. "We cannot explain it, actually."

"It was a very true likeness," Margaret explained. "I apologize for any suffering my mistake may have caused."

Mrs. Price huffed and pulled back her shoulders. "I cannot see how she looked 'just like you'." The neighbour appeared content to keep the blame directed at Margaret. "I mean, goodness, no two people appear the same, not unless they be twins, which is very unlikely. Most twins die a few days after birth. They are so scrawny and thin. They hardly stand a chance." The woman shook her head. "And we all know Miss Fannie Mae is not a twin. Isn't that right, Mrs. Harris?"

Margaret followed Mrs. Price's gaze to Mrs. Harris and realized the woman did not look well. Her grip went slack in Fannie Mae's hand and her gaze became unfocused.

"Mama?" Fannie Mae adjusted her spot on the floor to look at her mother squarely.

"Mrs. Price, I thank you for your assistance today," Mrs. Harris said, turning to her neighbour with direct purpose. "I appreciate you stopping by as soon as you heard the news. I would like to have a word with my daughter alone, if you please."

Mrs. Price looked genuinely shocked at the prospect of leaving, especially when the air was so ripe for salacious gossip.

Mrs. Harris gave a forced smile. "I shall call upon you if I require any further assistance."

Pulling her shoulders back, Mrs. Price stood. "Very well, Winifred. You know I am always at your service," she said, smoothing out the folds of her skirt. She crossed the sitting room and disappeared in the hall. Mrs. Harris quickly came to her feet and joined her friend at the door.

Margaret's gaze found Fannie Mae's. "I shall depart as well," she said, coming to her feet. "I'll give you and your mother some time to talk."

"Margaret, no." Fannie Mae grabbed Margaret's hand as if to prevent her from leaving.

"It's not my place. You mother wishes for privacy."

They heard the front door close but before Margaret could find her way to the hall Mrs. Harris returned. "Goodness no, my dear," she said directly to Margaret. "Please sit. My daughter has said nothing but the nicest things about you. I have no concerns regarding your loyalties."

Fannie Mae smiled, a look of 'I told you so' spreading over her face.

Once they were all settled back into their seats, Mrs. Harris turned to her daughter, who now sat beside her on the sofa. "Fannie Mae, I have something to tell you," she said.

Fannie Mae looked on with terrified anticipation. What could Mrs. Harris possibly have to say to her daughter? Margaret wondered. By all accounts, the Harrises were a typical Scottish family, mother, father, and an only child. It was clear, based upon what Fannie Mae had already confided and the look of trepidation that now spread over her features, that she had expected none of the subterfuge and secrecy that her mother now displayed.

Mrs. Harris's words did not spring forth easily. She expelled a steadying breath before pressing her lips together. "Fannie Mae, you are aware your father was a foundling, yes?"

"Yes, of course. He told me when I was a child." She turned to Margaret, as if embarrassed. Not that Margaret cared very much about it. Some may have been wary of orphans, but Margaret's mother had been a patron of a rather large orphanage back home. Margaret was raised with a strong notion of charity and was never taught that foundlings were degenerates, as others had been.

"Father told me foundlings are the best kinds because they are strong and resilient and will love you with all the strength in their hearts without being forced to by blood connection. And it's true, Mama. He loved you with everything he had."

Mrs. Harris smiled.

"It warms me to think that I was his only blood relative, something no one else could claim." Fannie Mae's face fell when she took in the expression on her mother's face. A look of apology and hesitation.

The room fell silent as the realization hit Fannie Mae. "Mama?"

Margaret's eyes welled up with tears as she watched her friend's heart break right before her eyes.

"Fannie Mae, my dear, you were one of the first babies born at Wendall Hall," Mrs. Harris said, squeezing her daughter's hand so she couldn't pull away. "The woman who gave birth to you had two children that day, two girls—"

Fannie Mae struggled against her mother's grip, finally pulling her hand free. She recoiled, inching away from her mother, a look of shock and sadness overtaking her face. "Don't..." she warned. Her curiosity stopped her from saying anymore. She wanted to know and didn't want to know at the same time.

"Two beautiful girls," Mrs. Harris continued, pulling a strand of loose hair away from her daughter's face and tucking it behind her ear. As if repulsed, Fannie Mae turned her body away from her mother's and nearly scooted to the farthest end of the sofa.

Margaret saw tears welling up in Mrs. Harris's eyes as well, but the older woman remained calm, almost resigned to the outcome. "Violet knew your father's history," she continued. "He had made himself an ardent supporter of her desire to make Wendall Hall into a place for wayward mothers. A place to facilitate healthy adoptions. Almost as soon as it opened she informed us of an expectant mother and asked us if we would be interested in providing a home for a little one. We did not find out until you had been with us for a few weeks that there had been another, a twin. Your father had said had he known, he would have accepted both of you... despite our limited means."

If Fannie Mae was listening she made no indication. She sat still as a statue at the end of the sofa, her gaze unfocused, her body unmoving.

"I had never wished to tell you," Mrs. Harris said. "Your father wanted you to know, but I just couldn't bear the thought of... of you knowing. Perhaps it was selfish of me," she continued, choking back tears as she watched her daughter's reaction. "I wanted to keep you all for myself."

"Are you telling me, the woman we found today"—sniffles interrupted Fannie Mae's words—"the woman could possibly be my twin sister?"

Mrs. Harris gave an exhale and nodded before closing her eyes.

A fresh round of wails escaped Fannie Mae then, an unmistakable agony that sent Margaret to Fannie Mae's side. She would have tried to console Mrs. Harris as well were she not seated so far away. Margaret sat next to her friend and placed a hand on Fannie Mae's knee.

"I am so sorry, Fannie Mae," Margaret said. She looked to Mrs. Harris then with marked sympathy. "I have nothing but compassion for you, Mrs. Harris," she said. "It cannot be easy to hold a secret for so long."

"You haven't any idea how many times I wished to tell you," Mrs. Harris said. Her words came out in fits and starts, grief and regret lacing her tone and stunting her movements. "I should have told you. I see now how much pain it has caused."

Mrs. Harris waited for a reply from Fannie Mae, perhaps hoping for some understanding or conciliatory words.

Nothing came. Margaret was too busy holding Fannie Mae's hand and rubbing her back that she did not notice Mrs. Harris had stood until the woman was crossing the room and heading for the door. Seconds later they heard hurried footfalls on the wood stairs and a door closing above them on the second floor.

"How can she do this to me, Margaret?" Fannie Mae said, aware that they were alone. "How could she allow me to believe I was Father's blood? I clung to that belief as a way to mourn his death. I believed he lived on through me."

"He does," Margaret said. "He does. We are not the product of our genes as much as we are products of the love that raises us."

Margaret's words seemed to have little to no effect. It was some time before Fannie Mae looked up from her hands, revealing ruddy cheeks and a swollen nose. "The woman was my sister, Margaret," she said. "My twin."

Margaret nodded.

"And she was killed. My sister was killed. Why, Margaret? Why would someone do this?"

Margaret tightened her embrace of Fannie Mae, pulling her close and resting a chin on Fannie Mae's quivering shoulder. "I don't know," she said, softly.

But I am certainly going to do my best to find out.

Chapter 9

When Margaret left Mrs. Harris's home an hour or so later Fannie Mae was close behind her.

"Are you sure you don't wish to stay for your mother's sake?" Margaret asked, turning to Fannie Mae on the stoop. Despite the hesitation evident on her face, Fannie Mae nodded. She glanced to a second-storey window. "I would like to return to Wendall Hall," she said, unable to meet Margaret's gaze. "There are a few questions I would like to ask Mrs. Bane."

Margaret saw a determination in Fannie Mae's features she had never seen before. The girl appeared resolute in her actions, neither asking permission nor expecting resistance. Margaret felt compelled to oblige.

They walked in silence to the main street of Helmsworth, spying the Wendall Hall carriage farther down. A train whistle sounded, bringing their attention to the station. The platform was awash with townsfolk returned from their jobs in Edinburgh. For Margaret the day had ended before it scarcely began.

"Is it truly so late in the day?" Margaret asked, her steps slowing.

Among the throng Margaret saw Jonas, descending the locomotive steps to the platform. She recognized a few Helmsworth residents at the ready, luring those who had been away in the city to their circle, promises of titillating gossip on their lips. A local man caught Jonas's arm and drew him in. Margaret watched helplessly, quickening her steps toward her husband, as the tale of the morning's discovery reached his ears. All happy anticipation drained from his face as he listened to the tale. Goodness knew what he was being told. Margaret felt the soft snow give way beneath her feet, as if pulling her backward from her direction of travel like rock-free sand on a beach. She pressed forward. Fannie Mae was matching her pace behind her but she too found the way difficult.

Margaret could see the look of concern on her husband's face, a look that morphed into worry and then fear as he listened. She couldn't allow him to believe she was harmed, not after all they had survived. Closer, she raised her arm, exposing her bare hand to the cold, and waved for him. "Jonas!" she called out. "Jonas!" Her voice was drowned out by the hum of the steam engine. A whistle sounded and was followed by a blast of compressed air at each wheel. She hurried her steps, ignoring the pain in her calves and thighs as she struggled against the snow.

"Jonas!"

Finally, he heard her and looked up, his face alighting brilliantly, his worry vanquished. He came toward her, his longer gait having better effect on the terrain. He divided the distance between them and dropped his medical bag in the snow before scooping her up in his arms.

"There is so much I need to tell you," she said into the warmth of his neck. She felt him squeeze her one notch tighter before allowing her body to slide down his front to the ground once again. She could see the remnants of worry on his face as he looked over her. "I don't know what you've been told," she said.

"Only that a woman has been killed at Wendall Hall," he said, closing his eyes to the thought. "My first thought was of you, thinking perhaps Eloise... it's impossible, I know," he said with a breathy air, "but the mind wanders to such things."

Margaret nodded. How many times had her own mind pondered such possibilities? Eloise was safely contained at Calton Jail and would be held for many years. They'd be informed of her release, Jonas had made sure of it, when the time came, but that did not stop Margaret from continually looking over her shoulders, peering nosily into dark rooms and assessing contents of large-sized cupboards.

"Another rumour persists," Margaret said, turning to Fannie Mae, who waited a few paces behind her. "The town is saying the murdered is Fannie Mae," she explained. "There is basis for this rumour, however." She became aware of the growing crowd around them, flooding the street from the train station. "Come," she said, plucking his medical bag from the ground and handing it to him, "let us take Fannie Mae back to the Hall together. We shall explain everything along the way."

She slipped her arm through the crook of his elbow and leaned in gently, glad to have him at her side, especially after such a trying day.

~ ~

Together Margaret and Fannie Mae let Jonas in on the true events that had taken place at Wendall Hall, relaying most of it before Benson had emerged from the post office.

"Who do they believe the girl is?" Jonas asked, his warm breath sending a swirl into the air about them.

Margaret watched as Fannie Mae's gaze went to the groundskeeper. She gave Margaret a slight shake of her head before her gaze fell to the ground.

"I'll tell you our theory later," Margaret said quietly, so Benson could not hear. "That is, if Fannie Mae will allow it."

Margaret's friend nodded permission but said nothing verbally as Benson looked them over.

"Are we all heading back then?" he asked, eyeing Jonas sideways.

"If it's all right with you, Mr. Benson," Margaret said.

"Makes no never mind to me, Mrs. Davies," Benson said, clamouring into the front seat, "so's long as ye don't pummel the bread and six dozen eggs Mrs. Bane asked me to fetch her."

Gingerly, Margaret and Fannie Mae positioned themselves between the parcels while Jonas skirted the carriage and climbed into the front from the opposite side.

"This is a mighty fine pair, Mr. Benson," Margaret overheard Jonas say, and watched him gesture toward the horses.

"Yeah, s'pose."

"How much does a pair such as this fetch around here, do you think?"

Margaret smiled at her husband's cleverness. Keeping Benson occupied allowed her and Fannie Mae time to chat among themselves.

"I don't know how she had done it, Margaret," Fannie

Mae said at last, once the carriage was well on its way and the two men up front were in deep conversation regarding the horses. "How had she kept it from me all these years?"

Margaret shook her head, nearly at a loss for words. "Perhaps she worried you would try to find your birth mother."

"Had I known I had a twin I might just have," Fannie Mae said, pulling her arms tighter around her torso as if to block out the cold. "I never knew her, Margaret," she said. "I had spent years praying for a sister and I had one all along. Have you any idea how lonely my childhood had been?"

Margaret shook her head. She may have been sister-less but her connection with Peter had made up for it in spades. They were closer to each other than any other sibling group Margaret had known. She wanted to tell Fannie Mae that family included more than just blood relations. She wanted her to know that sisters could be anyone, not just those who had come from the same parentage. In the end, however, Margaret held her tongue. It was not the time, not while Fannie Mae was so newly grieved, not while the wounds remained so fresh.

"I would have given anything for a real sister," Fannie Mae said, her voice low. "I feel a loss so much deeper than the one I felt when my father died. I feel like half of me remains frozen alongside her." She looked to Margaret suddenly. "Does that make sense?"

Margaret nodded. "Yes, it does. I may not have experienced this but I understand how painful it must feel." She choked back tears for her friend, tears of empathy and heartache.

She felt Fannie Mae inch closer beside her on the bench, slipping her arm underneath Margaret's. "You are such a dear friend, Margaret," Fannie Mae said, lowering her head so her cheek rested on Margaret's shoulder. "I don't know how I would ever have gotten through this day without you."

☙ ❧

Wendall Hall looked just as it always had, tall and

steadfast against the vacant field of snow. There was no indication anything untoward had taken place that morning. The deputy chief and his constable were long gone, as was the carriage they used to transport the body to Edenhall Hospital in Musselburgh, some ten miles away.

Jonas helped Margaret and Fannie Mae step down from the carriage. "Mr. Benson has agreed to transport me further on to Musselburgh," he said, giving Margaret an apologetic look. "I'd like to have a look at the body, to see what can be made of it."

"Then I'll come with you," Margaret said, stepping toward the carriage once more. Jonas stopped her with an outstretched hand.

"You should stay," Jonas said, lowering his hand to rest gently on Margaret's protruding belly. "It's far too cold and I'm afraid you've been out of doors too long."

"I'm not cold," she said in protest, returning her husband's stare. She hated the idea of him heading on without her. She was just as determined for answers as he was. Though he had once been agreeable to meet her demands, he seemed even less inclined now. It was the child, she realized. She wasn't only acting in her own best interests anymore, but also that of her unborn son or daughter.

"Margaret," he started, his face stoic and unmoved, "I should like it better if you would stay here, with Fannie Mae and the others. I shall take the train back before it gets too late."

Margaret could not bring herself to argue. But she did not immediately agree.

"Not to worry," he said quietly as he leaned in to kiss her forehead, "I shall tell you all that I discover."

Margaret gave a half smile at this. Somehow she had known he would. How many times had they shared discoveries and insights in the last year? Jonas, herself, and Peter had bonded over events such as these, murders and crimes, mysteries that needed to be solved. There was no need for her to worry that such a partnership would end now.

Before he turned back to the carriage he looked to Fannie Mae. "Look after her," he said. "Make sure she stays out of trouble." He gave Margaret a wink before climbing back into his seat. Margaret stepped back and felt Fannie Mae's hands encircle her arm as she drew close.

"Come, Margaret," she said, as the carriage slid over to the other side of the small hill. "I'm sure Mrs. Bane and Mrs. Gibson are in desperate need of some more help. For some reason Christmas is baby season."

They walked arm in arm along the drive to the house. It still didn't seem right to use the side door closest to the carriage house. Without saying a word, the pair came to a silent agreement and instead traipsed through the ankle-deep snow to the front door. Snow drifted down in a swirly cascade from the roof, littering them with what felt like frozen pinpricks on their faces. Clutching each other they bowed their heads and moved quickly, pushing open the door and nearly collapsing once inside.

Almost as soon as they entered the foyer, Margaret knew they weren't alone. She raised her gaze and saw two women standing a few paces inside, their coats, hats, and scarves and gloves already removed.

"Our apologies," Fannie Mae said, bowing her head and slipping past to the cloak closet.

Margaret could not move. There was something about the shape and form of the woman in front of her. The women were slow to turn but when they finally did, moving to see who stood behind them, Margaret's face lit up with recognition.

"Bethany!"

As soon as she spoke the word she wished she could choke it back. They weren't supposed to admit recognition of anyone who required their services. As her childhood friend from London turned, revealing a very round and expectant silhouette, Margaret realized she had committed an unforgivable gaff.

Fannie Mae stood at the cloak closet entrance, her gaze divided between the two clients and Margaret behind them.

Margaret's face blanched and she closed her eyes to steady her racing heart. "I'm so sorry. I thought you were someone I knew," she said, unwrapping her scarf from around her neck. "I've only recently moved from London, and I was excited at the thought of seeing a familiar face."

Margaret kept her gaze steady on Bethany's as she moved about peeling off her muff and unbuttoning her coat. "I see now I was mistaken," she added as she slipped by them in the hall.

"No harm done," Bethany's companion said, raising her chin slightly as Margaret passed.

"Have you been greeted by someone?" Fannie Mae asked.

"Yes, thank you," Bethany said, her eyes darting to Margaret and then forced back to Fannie Mae. "Mrs. Violet Bane is ensuring my accommodations are ready."

Fannie Mae nodded. "Yes, of course." She looked to Margaret, who wanted nothing more than to hide in the cloakroom, hidden among the coats, shawls, and boots. "My name is Fannie Mae and my friend here is Margaret. If there is anything either of you need we'd be most happy to assist," she explained.

Pretending to fiddle with the positioning of her coat, Margaret watched the opening of the door out the corner of her eye until Violet returned and offered to show the women to their room. As Bethany passed, her head turned to the open door and her eyes met Margaret's before snapping forward. Margaret closed her eyes, berating herself for being so careless.

"Is she a friend of yours?" Fannie Mae asked quietly, turning to Margaret.

Margaret nodded. "From London," she said. "We grew up together."

"They both seem very... upper crust," Fannie Mae said, sneaking a peek down the hall.

"Oh yes, very. Our families were very close."

"Really?" Fannie Mae's eyebrows shot up. "Imagine your family hobnobbing with a family like that."

"Why is that so unbelievable?" Margaret asked.

"Didn't you say your brother was a surgeon?"

Margaret's face fell. She had forgotten. Fannie Mae didn't know about Margaret's other brother, the fourth Earl of Montcliff, and the vast fortune and lands he managed as part of the Marshalls' legacy. As far as Fannie Mae was concerned, Margaret was the wife of a surgeon and the sister of a surgeon, not an heiress with access to an outrageous fortune. Not that the fortune was available to her now. Since her father died the month before, her brother, Daniel, had refused to release any of her funds, money that had been promised to her in their father's will. A dowry had been earmarked, and more besides for her own comfort. These contingencies were put in place years before. Had her father been well in the end, or even aware of her intentions to elope with Jonas, he'd most assuredly have written her out of the family arrangements. Even now she hadn't any idea what would become of it all.

Most days Margaret tried not to think about it. When it came down to it, she was Margaret Davies, the wife of a surgeon and no longer Margaret Marshall. That Margaret may as well just be a different person entirely. She bore no resemblance to the Margaret she was that day, the Margaret who lived in a small cottage, who held a nursing position at Wendall Hall, the Margaret who was months away from nappy changes and late-night feedings. For all intents and purposes, Margaret Marshall no longer existed and it was something Margaret wasn't all that torn up about.

"It's a bit difficult to explain," Margaret said.

"Goodness, Margaret," Fannie Mae said. "You are such a woman of mystery."

Chapter 10

In an effort to avoid further contact with Bethany and her companion, Margaret decided to head to the nursery, while Fannie Mae headed off to find Violet. "She must know something about my birth," Fannie Mae had said before they parted ways at the bottom of the stairs. "I cannot let another minute go by without knowing everything."

Margaret hadn't known what to say. She knew that Daniel had been happier believing he was their mother and father's first child together. It had gutted him considerably when he found out he was the result of their mother's affair. Margaret feared any answers Fannie Mae gleamed from Violet would only bring about further questions and, worst of all, it would never provide peace. But Margaret understood she had to know. Were Margaret in her shoes she'd want to know the truth even if it were a painful truth.

With Fannie Mae heading up the stairs, Margaret turned to the nursery door and leaned in close, listening through the wood for indication of what awaited on the other side. Then she slowly turned the knob, careful to make the least amount of noise as she entered.

Mrs. Gibson's face alighted at the sight of her. She was seated near the window, a small babe in her arms, sound asleep. "There's no need to be quiet, child," Mrs. Gibson told Margaret as she sneaked across the room, mindful of each creak and groan of the floorboards. "These wee ones sleep like the dead." She gestured for a chair opposite her, indicating for Margaret to take a seat.

Margaret realized the child was Christina, the one she had attended the evening before.

"I saw yer husband," Mrs. Gibson said, smiling slyly, "at the road just now."

"He's headed to Musselburgh to see what can be learned from the body."

Mrs. Gibson huffed. "I can't say much can be learned now. As the saying goes, Dead men tell no tales."

"But that's not entirely true," Margaret said rather quickly. "A lot can be learned, if you know how to look for the clues. My brother allowed me to assist with a post-mortem once. It wasn't that difficult, not as difficult as they all make it seem to be."

Mrs. Gibson raised her eyebrows, and looked as if she could laugh but was restraining herself. "Look at ye. Never did I peg you for a bluestocking." She looked at her sideways. "You sure you ain't never had a hankering to be a doctor like yer husband?"

Margaret wasn't ready to admit the thought had crossed her mind.

"There was a woman, you know, not long ago—well, actually, she were born a woman but she didn't stay that way fer long. Her real name was Margaret, now that I think of it. Fancy that!"

Margaret smiled.

"She attended the Edinburgh Medical School and then joined the Army."

"As a woman?" Margaret nearly jumped to the edge of her seat.

"Oh no. No, she disguised herself as a man and changed her name to Barry. Was it John? James?" Mrs. Gibson shook her head, deciding it didn't matter. "She used the name of her uncle who left her a large fortune. Seems a strange way to pay tribute to the man, if you ask me. She died a few years ago now, having lived as a man for nearly fifty years."

"I'd never heard such a story," Margaret confessed.

"Oh, they don't talk about it. The Army was quite put out about the whole affair. It was very scandalous. I only knows cuz my cousin works at the university, a porter you see, and one of the professors let it slip. They'll never admit it, though, that one of their best students in the last century was a woman. It's much easier for them to believe he were merely a short, smooth-faced man and not a rather intelligent, if conniving, young woman."

"Most men believe women incapable of being doctors. They say we haven't the stomach."

"Oh hogwash! I'ze seen enough bile and blood in a single hour that'd turn any doctor's stomach. No, Margaret, don't believe 'em. If ye wants to go and they won't let you, I say there's more ways than one to get the job done."

A knock sounded at the door. When Margaret looked she was surprised to see Violet slipping her way in. "Mr. and Mrs. Sinclair have arrived to take their wee one home," she said excitedly.

Margaret and Mrs. Gibson slid from their chairs as the adoptive couple entered the room. With the sleeping baby in her arms, Mrs. Gibson stepped forward. In unison the couple's faces alighted when they took in the sight of their child.

"Can I hold her?" Mrs. Sinclair asked, putting forth her arms to accept the swaddled baby. Mrs. Gibson slowly facilitated the exchange, easing the bundle into the arms of its new mother.

"We have some blankets for you to use to transport the young'un home," Violet explained.

"Oh we have a number of blankets to wrap her in," Mr. Sinclair explained. "Mary wouldn't leave the house without bringing nearly every blanket we own," he said, chuckling.

"It's only because it's so cold and we have such a way to travel," Mrs. Sinclair said, without taking her eyes from her new baby. "Thank you, everyone," she said, suddenly looking up, "for taking such good care of my baby."

"Of course," Mrs. Gibson said. "She's a sleeper. I can already tell."

Mrs. Sinclair smiled.

"By chance, have you thought of any names for her?" Margaret asked.

Both parents looked up. "We had thought of calling her Mary," Mr. Sinclair said with a noncommittal shrug.

"I'm not too fond of the idea," Mrs. Sinclair said. "I feel like she needs a name all her own."

"What about Christina?" Margaret suggested, recalling Maisie's wish.

"Christina." The name rolled off Mrs. Sinclair's tongue and was quickly followed by a smile. "Sounds lovely." She flashed a grateful smile to Margaret.

"Come, my dear, we should head home. I'd like to get there before it gets dark." Mr. Sinclair guided his wife from the room. Before Violet followed them into the hallway she winked to Margaret.

"Well played, Mrs. Davies," she said.

Margaret beamed. "Mrs. Bane, I think I should inform you that my husband has gone ahead to Musselburgh. He said he will tell us what he learns from the body."

Violet stopped and laid a hand on the doorframe as she looked back to her. "He needn't have bothered," she said, failing to mask her worry.

"It's our wish to help Fannie Mae discover the root of all this," Margaret said. "She deserves to know the truth."

Violet struggled to keep the pasted smile on her face. "I'm sure the police detectives have everything well in hand. You really shouldn't bother yourself, Margaret," she said. "In this case, I think it best to leave well enough alone." She left the room quickly after that, closing the door and leaving Margaret to wonder what exactly she had meant by that.

※ ※

The next twenty minutes passed in relative quiet. It was as if, as the sun set, Wendall fell asleep. No babies remained in the nursery and Mrs. Gibson's youngest son, Luke, was spending the day with his father and siblings, which gave Margaret and Mrs. Gibson the opportunity to give the room a thorough clean. They stripped all the cots of their linen, and set a pile near the door and then together gave every surface a good scrub. Margaret worked at the windows while Mrs. Gibson was on her knees on the floor.

"The quiet won't last for long," Mrs. Gibson said, huffing over her quick movements with the scrub brush. "We had four more ladies come today. Two of them looked about to burst." She leaned back and brushed a strand of hair from her forehead with the back of her wrist. "What are ye doing, Margaret?"

Margaret pulled her hand back from the window, and looked over her work. The panes were small squares and each one needed individual attention. The small panes in a relatively large window box was an economic decision rather than a labour-conscious one. If one pane was broken only the small square would need replacing instead of a larger pane of glass. But this design, though economical, made difficult work of an already tedious job. Margaret knew she wasn't performing her duty well. Each time she pulled her rag away she saw streaks, even in the failing light. It did not matter how many times she ran the cloth over the window, streaks always reappeared.

"Use the newspaper," Mrs. Gibson said, from her spot on the floor.

"Newspaper?" Margaret eyed the small pile of newsprint next to the bucket of warm water Mrs. Gibson had fetched for her.

"You wash the window with the cloth and then use the newspaper to give it a sheen."

Margaret didn't bother to hide her look of confusion. She had never been expected to clean before and never really paid much attention to how the servants went about their chores. Had the servants at Marshall House used newspaper? Certainly, Father regularly consumed enough of them to keep the entire house pristine, if this was truly how it was done.

Soon Mrs. Gibson was on her feet and at Margaret's side. Without annoyance or frustration, the woman showed Margaret how to wash the windows properly.

"If ye plan on passing for merely a doctor's wife, ye best to learn a thing or two about seeing to the household, to instruct your staff at the very least."

Margaret lowered her gaze to the cloth in her hand, aware of the warm soapy water rolling down her wrists and disappearing into her sleeve. She couldn't help but think of all the women who must have washed the windows of her room over the years. How many times had Margaret looked out over the rear yard, or the front street back home, her view unmarred by the soot and grime found both inside and out? She had never noticed the women. Any of them. She barely noticed how clean the windows had been, but clean they were. They must have been, for if they weren't she was sure her father would have noticed and complained to the housekeeper. Margaret felt embarrassed for her oversight, for never once having considered how the things in her life came to be cleaned, pressed, and made just so. She also felt embarrassed for never having done any of these things herself. It was as if she were an owner of slaves, the owner of bone-weary women who had no other choice in life but to cook and clean for Margaret Marshall, whose only true difference from any of them was her hereditary fortune.

A noise from across the hall broke her from her reverie. A door shut harshly, and then muffled shouts followed, somehow finding their way into the nursery.

"I've worked for you for three years!" Fannie Mae's voice was punctuated with frustration and, as far as Margaret could tell, hurt.

"I should have never hired you on," Violet Bane was heard answering.

Margaret shot a glance to Mrs. Gibson, who also heard the conversation and halted her task as well. Together they took steps toward the closed nursery door and listened, enraptured by the passionate words exchanged.

"I didn't realize who you were until you were already working here," Violet said.

"You could have told me I was a foundling," Fannie Mae said.

"It wasn't my place," Violet answered. "Parents are the ones who get to choose if and when to tell their children. It's not up to me."

"But you knew. You saw her dead in the snow and you knew who it was and you never said anything."

"It wasn't my pl—"

"You keep saying that!"

"It's true! Your parents deserve privacy just as much as any of our other clients."

A moment of silence followed. As Margaret listened she could make out the faint sound of Fannie Mae weeping. Margaret turned to Mrs. Gibson. "Maybe we should go over. I think Fannie Mae maybe be crying."

Mrs. Gibson shook her head but the look on her face betrayed her worry. Margaret wasn't sure if she meant they shouldn't intervene or if she was made uncomfortable by the confrontation.

"Who is she? I need to know her name," Fannie Mae asked, her voice barely audible between the two doors that separated her and her sniffling.

"I cannot tell you."

"The woman is dead! My sister! Her family must be

notified."

Margaret strained to listen and eventually opened the door to the nursery to lessen the barriers. She remained at the threshold, however, and bent her head to listen. If Fannie Mae came out, Margaret would be ready to console her.

"Did you tell the police officers at least?" Fannie Mae pressed.

"No, I didn't think it was my—"

"Your place! I understand. A woman is dead and her family... her adoptive family remains unaware while you sit here protecting your precious charity."

"Fannie Mae, it's not about Wendall Hall. It would have been better, for all of us, if this never happened, but there's nothing we can do for it now."

"Except find the person responsible." Again, quiet fell over the room. "Margaret says she's helped with things such as this before."

"Mrs. Davies is merely biding her time while waiting for her baby to arrive. She's a bored socialite, nothing more," Violet snapped.

Margaret's gaze went to Mrs. Gibson. She had heard the insult as well.

"Margaret is a dear friend, dearer than I have ever known. I hope she never finds out what you truly think of her."

Margaret heard the door to Violet's office snap open. She and Mrs. Gibson didn't have a chance to duck back into the nursery. When she looked up, Fannie Mae was staring back at her, eyes and nose red from crying. Behind her, not two paces away, stood Violet, a look of horror overcoming her features.

Fannie Mae glanced over her shoulder to Violet, her face displaying a look of censure.

Margaret felt overwhelmed. She could feel herself readying to cry and tried to push down the emotions that threatened to spill over.

"What do you think, Margaret, shall we call it a day then?" Fannie Mae asked. "The atmosphere feels chillier in here than it does out of doors."

Margaret nodded and before she could say anything else

Fannie Mae was whisking her down the hall to the cloakroom.

"I'm just a bored socialite then, am I?" Margaret asked, once they were finally outside and heading through the woods back to Helmsworth village.

The evening was crisp without a snowflake in the sky but the cold was ever present, nipping at all exposed skin and causing them to hurry their steps down the path.

"Pay no attention to her," Fannie Mae said, bristling against a gust of wind that had sprung up around them. "I don't think she realizes how good she had it with us at Wendall Hall. Why, I'm not so sure you and I should show up tomorrow. We'll see how she handles things without us then, won't we?"

Margaret chuckled at the thought. She and Jonas didn't need the money she earned but she was almost positive Fannie Mae and her mother depended on the funds a great deal.

"Maybe you should ask for some time off, just for the holidays," Margaret suggested. "Then you can get a fresh start in the new year."

"Maybe I should seek out a new position altogether," Fannie Mae said with an indignant huff. "Can you believe she had the gall to refuse telling me who my sister is? A sister who has already been struck from this world? What harm can it do anyone now? The woman is dead. I don't understand how Violet can live with herself."

Margaret didn't entirely understand it either. Given the circumstances, everything should be out in the open now.

"I don't know how we are going to find out anything about my birth family now," Fannie Mae said.

"Don't worry, Fannie Mae," Margaret said. "Jonas is finding out what he can. I'm sure a lead will make itself known before we know it."

Chapter 11

Edenhall Hospital was a two-storey building, nearly the smallest hospital Jonas had ever seen in his lifetime, and the room at the bottom of the basement stairs was no different. Large enough to hold a single body and not much more, the morgue was chilled to the point of being nearly frozen and provided little difference from the winter landscape outside. When Jonas arrived at the entrance the detectives were long gone, forcing him to call for the attention of a passing porter.

"Who is the doctor who oversees this room?" he asked quietly, as if the normal volume of his voice would risk waking the dead. His question hadn't been made for more than two seconds before a head peeked around the doorframe of a room farther down.

"Who wants to know?" a young man asked, his tone gruff.

"Dr. Jonas Davies, from Edinburgh Medical School."

If the question had been posed four years prior Jonas wouldn't have been able to answer so confidently. Despite graduating from medical school at the top of his class, an honour he shared equally with Margaret's brother Peter, his impoverished upbringing made him meek and timid when challenged directly. At least on the inside. Outwardly he had played along with the best of them, the boys from well-off families, giving as good as they gave, but internally he wondered if they could tell he hadn't eaten much in the last three days or that he'd just spent his last shilling on a drink with the boys, the last of money that was supposed to last a fortnight. He could do nothing to hide the patches on his knees or the overlong hair that had required a trim twice over. He had developed a persona, though, a persona of carefree nonchalance, someone unaffected by whether someone liked him or disliked him. He'd modeled this character off of Peter, and others, young men with money and connections. Young men who had grown up commanding things of others and expecting obedience. It was a practiced skill—confidence. One that had never come easy to him, not after his special commendations and certainly not after being falsely accused of murder, an accusation that dogged him still.

"A doctor, huh?" The man stepped out of the room. He waved at the porter as he walked toward them. "That'll do, Drummond." The man presented a hand to Jonas. "Dr. John Cameron," he said. It was clear he got a kick out of his honorific title. Dr. Cameron looked terribly young, young enough to make Jonas wonder if the man was twelve when he entered medical school.

"You have an interest in our latest arrival?" Dr. Cameron asked, clicking his tongue and hopping up on his heels as if he personally had something to do with its presence there. "I mean, is Edinburgh interested, by chance?"

"No, the woman is related to a woman my wife works with."

"Oh." The man nodded as he led Jonas back into the morgue room. "Works, does she? And here I thought all the doctors at Edinburgh made enough their wives don't have to work."

"She chooses to work," Jonas clarified.

"Does she now?"

Doubt was written on the man's face. Women didn't choose to work. They did so because they had to and it was a stain on any man whose wife was forced to toil outside the home. It was clear Dr. Cameron believed Jonas wasn't displaying enough shame for the state of his marriage. What was also as equally clear was the fact that Jonas felt no need to defend his or his wife's decisions. Seeing this, Dr. Cameron exhaled, raising his eyebrows to highlight the awkwardness, and reverted his attention back to the body.

"Well...Given that your wife knows this woman's sister, perhaps you can help me identify her?"

"I'm afraid that isn't possible," Jonas said, meeting the man's gaze. "Not at present."

Dr. Cameron returned his gaze, unsure.

"It's a bit of a complicated situation. I just wanted to see if there was anything apparent, something I can return with in regards to how she passed and the circumstances surrounding it."

"I haven't done up my report. She just arrived, so I've barely done more than a precursory glance." Dr. Cameron pulled the sheet back from the woman's head, folding it in a double layer over her chest. The woman was still fully clothed. She wore a thick wool coat in dark green and the collar at her neck was lace, but beyond this Jonas could not see.

One thing was glaringly evident. The woman had suffered a deep gash to the back of her head. Cameron touched the sides of her face and turned the cranial so Jonas could see the injury in full detail.

"As you can see, cause of death is rather apparent," Dr. Cameron said. He stood back and watched as Jonas drew closer. "She slipped on ice and hit her head, I'd wager. A single blow."

Jonas looked around for tools. "Tweezers?" he asked finally.

"Oh." Seconds later Cameron returned with a solid, pristine pair.

"Can you drop the light a bit?" Jonas asked, leaning in.

Sure enough, Dr. Cameron was able to lower the overhead light, which helped illuminate the woman's injury. "How confident are you with that wager?" Jonas asked after a moment.

Dr. Cameron blanched, seeing the seriousness in Jonas's face. Gambling had once been a big part in Jonas's life and there was still a gambling itch in him.

"What do you mean? Clearly, she suffered a blow to the head."

"She was hit twice," Jonas said after a moment. He looked up to see the doubt on Dr. Cameron's face. "The first blow hit here," he said, indicating an impact wound that didn't penetrate into the skull. "She fell forward and then the assailant hit her again here." Jonas used the tips of the tweezers to highlight a more penetrating wound, slightly off centre from the first but still in the same general area. As Jonas studied the indents, the circumstances became clear. The first blow knocked the woman unconscious. The second blow was delivered when she was no longer moving and the ground on the other side braced her, which resulted in a deeper impact.

"She didn't just fall and hit her head," Jonas said. "She was struck. Deliberately."

Dr. Cameron looked on but said nothing as Jonas pulled back a flap of scalp slightly. He didn't want to do too thorough an examination, not just then. "Are there any other wounds on her?" Jonas asked. Without waiting for a response, he pulled back the sheet to examine her clothes.

"No, not that I could tell." Dr. Cameron looked torn between asking Jonas to leave and asking him to assist with the exam. "There was some blood apparent on her mouth and nostrils."

Jonas looked over the woman's clothes. The hem of her dress was crinkly to the touch, still damp with mud that was ground into the very underside of the fold. Her shoes were good quality, black with a slight heel. He tipped her foot to the side and saw some thin orange lines near her sole. Jonas leaned in and brushed his thumb over the lines and realized they were dried pine needles. When he looked at the undersides of her shoes he found a few more. The snow she had treaded through must have washed any other evidence away. Everything looked in order. As if she had indeed been walking and merely slipped and struck her head.

Jonas looked to the woman's torso. Her stomach appeared flat. "I need to know if she was with child," he said. "And how far along she was into her pregnancy."

"With child?"

Jonas nodded.

"Does she have a husband then?"

Jonas raised the woman's left hand, flashing an empty ring finger to the doctor.

"Oh."

"I realize it's late but can you do this first thing in the morning and get word to me in Edinburgh?" Jonas asked, searching his inside breast pocket for his calling card. Printed on it was his name, his position at the university, and the location of his office.

"Yes, of course," Cameron said, accepting the card Jonas gave him. "I'll start once I have enough sunlight. Should I not send the report to Deputy Chief Kelly?"

Jonas offered a puzzled look.

"If you are spearheading the investigation—"

"I'm not spearheading anything," Jonas said. "See that Deputy Chief Kelly gets his report. I am merely acting on behalf of the family. Consider your part a professional courtesy."

Dr. Cameron nodded. "Yes, of course. I will see what I can do."

"Thank you."

As Jonas left he found himself surprised at the ease with which Dr. Cameron took him at his word. Jonas wasn't so used to such trust, not anymore. Were the woman sent to Edinburgh he'd have had to fight more rigorously for access and further still for information. His interaction with Dr. Cameron reminded him how easy it had once been when his reputation hadn't been clouded with suspicion. He hadn't killed Professor Frobisher and he, Peter, and Margaret had gathered ample evidence to prove it, but because no one at the Edinburgh staff had seen Giles's confession the doubt remained and Jonas was placed under careful watch. No one trusted him despite the fact he had done absolutely nothing wrong. If it weren't for Margaret, the last two months would have been unbearable.

She deserved better than this. Better than a husband fallen from grace. Better than dubious stares and whispers in society parlours. They both deserved a fresh start so that all interactions were as easy as the one he just had with Dr. Cameron. But how and where exactly would such a fresh start begin?

        ❧ ☙

When Jonas arrived home a warm glow from the windows invited him inside. Chilled from the journey in the open carriage, he was thankful for the warm fire and the smell of dinner that enveloped him when he entered the door.

"You're back!" Margaret popped into the hall, a welcoming smile on her face. She eagerly took his coat and hat before planting a soft kiss on his lips. His skin was practically frozen compared to her warmth. "I'm afraid supper isn't much," she said. "I figured soup was safer after the roast I burned last week."

Jonas moved his medical bag to the crook of the stairs and followed her into the kitchen.

"I wasn't exactly sure what to put in the soup so I made my best guess." She walked to the stove and took up a large ladle to stir her creation. The pot's contents nearly spilled over the rim as she turned it.

"How much did you make?" Jonas asked, easing toward the stove to have a look inside.

"Too much, I think, for just the two of us," she admitted, biting her lower lip.

Jonas couldn't help but smile at her efforts. She hadn't been raised for this, not as other women had. Margaret had enjoyed a life of leisure, attending garden parties and theatre premiers. Her family employed nearly three dozen servants divided between their London house and their country house in Kent. With so many hands eager to please Lord Marshall and his family, there was simply no need for Margaret to learn any of the things other young ladies did. Instead, she learned to draw, dance, and flirt. She could speak three languages: English, French, and Latin, and recite any number of different poems, but these skills were useless in the countryside when balls and garden parties were few and far between. Not that the Davies would be getting many invites, not these days and not of the same caliber Margaret had become accustomed to.

There was some culinary instruction, Margaret once confessed. While she lived in the countryside with her mother, she had made jam collecting the berries from the vines and trudging them into the kitchens. "Cook did most of the work but Peter and I watched mesmerized," she had said. "I became very proficient with a knife cutting the greens off the strawberries without wasting any of the fruit." She had beamed excitedly at the memory of it.

"Excellent, as long as we can make jam we will be well fed," Jonas had teased.

In truth, he admired her tenacious efforts, her willingness to adjust her expectations for the sake of a life together. There was no hope of him ever being able to reproduce the luxury she had come to know. But he knew, in the grand scheme of it, they'd be happier for it.

After dinner Jonas helped her with the washing up, ignoring her numerous remarks that he needn't bother assisting her. He had been taking care of himself well enough for a number of years, and washing a few dishes as a married man certainly wouldn't kill him.

She eyed him sideways as she stood at the sink. A smile spread over her lips, a smile of anticipation. "So, husband," she said, "what did you discover in Musselburgh?"

She looked so adorable when she was trying to be coy. "Not much," he said, trying to keep a straight face. He was facing the cupboard and was glad he didn't have to face her. She'd suss out his teasing and win him over within a heartbeat.

"Not much?"

When he turned to face her, she was staring directly at him, a fist on her hips and quizzical expression on her face.

"Our mystery woman died from a blow to the head." He patted the space behind his ear to show her where the injury was. He walked back to the counter to dry another dish. "Dr. Cameron believed she slipped on ice and fell."

"What do you believe?"

"I believe she was hit twice. The second blow was more powerful than the first." He raised his gaze from the rinsed bowl in his hand. Margaret had stopped washing.

"Were both wounds in the same place?"

"Just about."

"If she was struck once she would have moved, or turned?"

Jonas shook his head. "I believe the first blow knocked her to the ground. The second was delivered while she lay unconscious. That was most likely the blow that killed her."

Margaret nodded, letting his words and descriptions sink in.

"I imagine we can prove my theory by examining any structural damages to the opposite side of her head. There'd at least be a facial fracture or crack to indicate where her face met the walkway...I'm sorry. You did not wish to hear all the details." He glanced to her burgeoning stomach and wondered if he'd speak so freely if their baby sat nearby at the kitchen table.

"No, I'm alright," Margaret answered. "I want to know these things so I can better help Fannie Mae. It's just…"

Jonas waited, using his cloth to wipe the bowl that was already bone dry.

Margaret turned to look him in the eyes. "I saw her," she said. "She lay exactly as you would expect given your description. I've never seen such a thing. Not even when my mother died. Her image has been following me around the entire day and now to think of how it all came to be…" She closed her eyes. "It's awful," she said. "Just plain awful."

She raised her hands to her face, crying into them, as if it were the first round of true tears shed for the woman who passed. Jonas laid the bowl and cloth down on the counter and encircled his wife in his arms.

"What if she were pregnant?" she asked, her voice muffled among the layers of clothing and the tight embrace. "What if she had come for assistance and someone was afraid she would tell? What if it were the father of the baby that killed her?"

Jonas closed his own eyes against the thought, a thought that was both horrendous and yet possible at the same time.

"Look at me," Margaret said suddenly, pushing him away gently and tracing the undersides of her cheeks to wipe away her tears. "Crying over someone I didn't even know. You and Peter have seen and heard worse, I am sure. I've seen worse." She laughed nervously and stroked the crest of her stomach. "Goodness, it's like this baby is playing with me. I don't recognize myself anymore." She looked up to Jonas then. "Is this normal?"

Jonas nodded. "I have heard it is. Women's hearts do soften after becoming mothers."

Margaret was not pleased with this. She returned to his embrace, wrapping her arms around him and pressing her cheek into his chest. "What about fathers? Don't fathers feel these changes?"

"Yes, my darling, I do believe they do."

After an hour of reading by lamplight in the parlour they

decided they were ready for bed. By the time Jonas had secured the doors and climbed the stairs to their bedchamber, Margaret had removed her petticoats and other hidden layers of underclothes and was perched on her side of the bed in her nightdress. While he undressed, she began the long process of pulling out her hair, searching out each pin, and then running her fingers through her curls as they cascaded over her shoulders. Even after a few months of marriage he had trouble not watching as she did it. He loved seeing her dark brown hair down and framing her sweet face.

"Something else happened today," she said after long last.

He could tell by the look on her face that whatever it was she was saddened by it.

"Actually, two things happened. After you and Arthur dropped us at the road I saw Bethany. You remember Bethany?"

"Yes, of course," Jonas admitted. "Your friend from London."

"She was admitted to Wendall Hall today."

Jonas paused. "Is she…"

Margaret nodded and closed her eyes. "And I made a huge mistake," she said.

Jonas went to her and took a seat on the edge of the bed directly in front of her.

"I saw her in the hall and I immediately called out to her. I'm not supposed to do that," she said. "We aren't supposed to admit we recognize anyone unless they admit they recognize us. You should have seen the look on her face. I could tell she was embarrassed."

"Of having an association with you?"

"No… well, yes, perhaps." She let out a deep breath as if resigned to say what had been on her mind, knowing he wouldn't be happy about it. "I haven't the slightest clue what Daniel has been saying about me, or Aunt Louisa, for that matter. I suppose they have been telling all their friends of my transgressions, marrying a man of the trade class. I can only imagine what they must think of me."

"The devil what they think of you. Peter has gone public regarding his medical training," Jonas countered. "Isn't deceit more scandalous than marrying for love?"

"Yes, but perhaps they are saying you tricked me, or that we only wed because of the baby."

"Let them think whatever they want," Jonas answered. "I'm not in the habit of living my life for the pleasure of others." He forced Margaret to look at him by lifting her chin gently with two fingers. "You are my wife, who I love and adore, and it doesn't matter what any of them believe about it."

Margaret smiled slightly at his words.

"I hope you didn't just marry *me* because of the baby?"

"Of course not!"

Jonas winked. "Just checking." He leaned forward and kissed her on the lips before getting up from the bed to finish undressing. "Don't think of Bethany. We have no need of fair-weather friends."

Margaret smiled at this.

"I wish her well, of course," Jonas said, "Especially given her troubles, but you needn't feel slighted, not when the one doing the slighting is in a scandalous position herself."

Margaret nodded. "I thought... well, I thought, what better time for a friend than when you are in need... scared as well, I imagine..."

"Exactly, my darling," Jonas said, pulling at the buttons at his collar. "She may come around in time, but if not, you'll know what sort of friendship you shared."

Margaret nodded. "You always have a way to make me feel better," Margaret said, settling down into the bedclothes.

"What was the other thing?" Jonas asked, pulling at his cufflinks.

"I'm sorry?"

"You said two things happened today. What was the other thing?"

Margaret looked reluctant to talk about it. "It's nothing I can't handle but... Mrs. Gibson and I heard Fannie Mae and Violet arguing this afternoon."

"About what?"

"About Violet not telling Fannie Mae she was a foundling. I can't help but agree with Violet. It wasn't her place to tell Fannie Mae such a thing. If her parents wanted her to know they would have told her."

"Even after the body of the woman was discovered?" Jonas asked.

"See, I don't know. Why would Violet keep such knowledge to herself? She said she hadn't even told the police."

"That is odd."

"Very odd. I've been turning it over in my mind all night. Violet has to know who adopted both Fannie Mae and her sister. A quick look at the records would allow us to at least inform her family that their daughter has died." Margaret closed her eyes. "But that's only half of it. At the end of the argument, Violet said I was just a bored socialite who was biding my time while waiting for my baby to be born."

"She said this?"

"Yes! I heard her. I didn't know what to say or do. It hurt to think that was how she felt about me. I felt like an apprentice in a way. I thought she was teaching me. Turns out she was just humouring me."

Jonas shrugged off his shirt, pulling carefully on the ends of his cuffs, and then wrapped it around his valet stand. When he looked to Margaret he saw how weary she was. It had been a difficult day from start to finish.

"Truth is, I don't know where I belong anymore. I no longer fit in with everyone I knew before. I feel like even my new friends will never truly accept me. And I feel so isolated out here from my family."

"I'd take you back to London if I could." Jonas pulled back the sheets and slid in beside her.

"Oh I know." Margaret rolled over and nestled herself against him. "It's not that. I'm merely adjusting. I've been trying to keep myself busy at the Hall so I don't have to think about it. When I'm here all alone I feel overwhelmed with homesickness and fear."

"Fear?"

Margaret placed a hand at the crest of her stomach. "What if something goes wrong?" she asked. "We nearly lost a mother last week. It's a wretched business, childbirth. I see woman after woman struggle for hours. I don't know if I have it in me. I'm not strong like they are."

Jonas held back a chuckle. "Oh yes you are, Margaret

Davies," he said. "You are the bravest and strongest of women. I've seen what you are made of and I am not scared in the least." He leaned forward and planted a kiss on her forehead. "You will be the best mother. I can see it in you already."

Chapter 12

Annalise said nothing disparaging about the rather large pot of soup remaining from the evening before, and of that Margaret was thankful. "Take some for your family," Margaret offered, knowing right well both she and Jonas would never finish it all before it spoiled.

The maid said nothing at first and instead inserted a spoon for a quick taste test. Margaret braced herself for a biting remark and was surprised when it never came.

A knock sounded at the door just as Margaret was about to ask Annalise for some assistance with her shoes, an everyday task that was becoming increasingly difficult as her pregnancy progressed.

Feeling quite frazzled and pressed for time, Margaret answered the door, tossing a hastily removed apron to the bottom step hidden behind the door.

"Mrs. Gibson, I'm so delighted you called." Margaret stepped aside, inviting her in, but Mrs. Gibson was quick to shake her head.

"I must be heading off, Mrs. Davies. Violet will be expecting me a'fore long." She stopped suddenly as if remembering the words they had both heard from Mrs. Violet. "Ye aren't put out by what Mrs. Bane said, are ye? I can assure you she is just tired, is all. Cranky. Happens to the best of us." She paused again, most likely seeing the look of unease on Margaret's face. "I could tell she felt dreadful after you and Miss Harris left yesterday evening."

"Did she say as much?"

"Well, no. I saw it in her face, like. She don't mean nothing by what she said. She were just flustered by her row with Miss Harris."

"I wasn't going to stay away all day," Margaret conceded, looking beyond Mrs. Gibson to the condition of the road beyond. "I just have a few things to ready for Christmas."

Mrs. Gibson seemed appeased by this. "Very well then," she said. "I only came because... well, I heard what Mrs.

Bane and Fannie Mae were fighting about. Am I to understand that Miss Harris and the woman we found yesterday were twins, unbeknownst to Fannie Mae?"

Begrudgingly, Margaret nodded. No doubt the entire town knew as much by then, thanks to the Harris's neighbour, Mrs. Price.

"Well, then I must admit it got me thinking of an incident that happened last week."

"Last week?"

"Yes, it were Sunday and Mrs. Violet and I were the only ones about. And I looked out the nursery window and saw Fannie Mae coming up the walk. Only I don't think it were Fannie Mae." Mrs. Gibson hesitated, catching her breath and perhaps organizing her words. "I waved out the window to her and even popped into the hall to give her a more formal greeting but..."

"She didn't behave so familiar?" Margaret guessed.

"Yes, I thought it strange at the time. Violet whisked her away, ushering her into her office quickly, and didn't say a word about it. I thought maybe Fannie Mae wasn't feeling so well, a little under the weather, so to speak."

Margaret nodded but her mind raced. If Mrs. Gibson had seen Fannie Mae's twin on Sunday, that must mean the woman had visited Wendall Hall more than once.

"Can you recall any other times such as these?" Margaret asked quickly.

"No, ma'am," Mrs. Gibson said. "Just the once. I thought I'd tell you on account of what's happened. Through the door, after they first went inside Violet's office, I heard Violet say 'Good morning, Emma,' and then she asked how the roads had been from Dunbar."

Margaret suppressed a smile. "This is wonderful, Mrs. Gibson." She reached out and grabbed Mrs. Gibson's hand, squeezing it with thanks.

"I ain't heard anything else," Mrs. Gibson said. "If I did I would tell you as I think you and Miss Harris are doing the right thing. It's a sin for a mother to not know when her child has died, an absolute sin. I hope you track down this woman's family and tell her what's happened, Violet Bane be damned." The woman's eyes grew wide at her choice of words. "I apologize Mrs. Davies... I..."

"It's all right, Mrs. Gibson. It isn't something I haven't heard before," Margaret said with a slight laugh. "I can tell you are quite convinced in this."

"I barely slept all night thinking on Emma's mother, not knowing her daughter had been found frozen in the snow. T'isn't proper for Mrs. Bane to hide information, especially from the police."

"I can assure you, I will see that Emma's mother is informed."

"There's a good girl," Mrs. Gibson said, touching a cold palm to Margaret's cheek. "I must be off," she said suddenly. "Will I see you at the Hall later?"

Margaret nodded. "Of course."

The woman smiled and was away before Margaret could say anything else.

"Is this about the dead woman business?" Annalise asked as Margaret closed the door.

She had not realized Annalise was standing behind her and she wondered how much of the conversation the maid had eavesdropped on. "I don't see how it's anything that concerns you," Margaret said evenly. She tried to pass her through the narrow doorway but the woman stood firm in place.

"It is my concern if there's a murderer about town killing innocent women," Annalise said, keeping her gaze.

"I don't believe there is anything to fear," Margaret answered. "In my experience, most murderers are people who are known to the victim. There is a specific reason for the killing." Finally, Margaret used her hand to nudge Annalise forward to the side slightly and was able to saddle by.

"In your experience?" Annalise turned to follow Margaret to the kitchen. "Exactly how much experience do you and Dr. Davies have in such things?"

"More than you'd imagine."

ಞ ✂

Margaret approached Fannie Mae's house with considerable trepidation. She couldn't help but think of Mrs. Harris, and the tribulations she had been having of late. Whatever her reasons for keeping her daughter's foundling status a secret Margaret had to believe there was a good reason. It must have been difficult for them, Mr. and Mrs. Harris, to want a child, to pray for a child, and be denied in all ways except adoption. Perhaps keeping this detail from Fannie Mae was a decision to keep the remembrances at bay, to rewrite history in their favour. Maybe they wished to avoid the inevitable questions or to save Fannie Mae the pain of rejection after realizing her birth mother had not wanted her. In truth, it didn't matter what their reasons were. As parents to a child, their child, they were entrusted with those kinds of decisions, and no one else.

Margaret knocked and the door was opened with her hand still on the iron knocker.

"I saw you coming up the lane," Fannie Mae said happily. She tugged Margaret inside. "I'm so glad you are here, Margaret. Everything is so grey and gloomy." She made a noise in her throat, disgust and angst all in one. "Mrs. Harris hasn't talked to me since yesterday, well, she's barely stepped out of her room, and I had to make breakfast for the boarders all by myself. She did come down but she's in no state to be seen by anyone so I told her I would handle it."

Margaret glanced to the stairs. "Is it so bad?"

Fannie Mae appeared far less concerned. "She'll be fine, I imagine. And it's not like she didn't do it to herself."

Margaret did not like this. The entire time she had known Fannie Mae it seemed as if she and her mother were close, sharing the sort of relationship Margaret wished she'd had with her own mother.

"Fannie Mae—"

Fannie Mae pretended she didn't hear her. "I just can't shake off my argument with Mrs. Bane." She pulled Margaret's muff away and held out her hand as if to accept her coat. "I still don't understand why she won't tell the police at least. Seems ridiculous to keep these things to ourselves. More people are involved than just me and the woman, you understand?"

Fannie Mae led her into the kitchen and began pouring two cups of tea straightaway.

"Oh yes, I understand," Margaret said. "That's actually why I've come. Mrs. Gibson stopped by. She said she thinks the woman's name is Emma and that she resides in Dunbar or thereabouts."

"Margaret!" Fannie Mae put down the teapot abruptly, a look of elation on her face.

"I haven't been able to confirm any of it," she said, trying to temper Fannie Mae's excitement. "We don't know how accurate this information is. I thought maybe you'd like to head over with me. We can see if we can find her family at least."

"Yes!" Fannie Mae was already reaching for her coat. "Yes, I'll come. We can take Annabelle and Queenie. Do you know how to ride sidesaddle?" Fannie Mae abandoned the tea and made for the door hallway as if to fetch her coat.

"Yes," Margaret said, trying to follow her movements.

"Good, we only have two saddles and if I ride sidesaddle I always feel like I am going to fall off." She pulled her coat from the hall stand and hurriedly worked to put it on. "Mama—I mean, Mrs. Harris—will only ride sidesaddle."

Margaret touched Fannie Mae's arm to gather her attention and lowered her voice. "Do you think you should be calling her that? She is your mother, if not your birth mother."

"Don't you think I should call her what I want, seeing as I was the one brought into the family unwillingly?"

"We are all brought into our families unwillingly," Margaret corrected gently.

Fannie Mae waved off her concern and grabbed her scarf and mittens. "Come along then," she said excitedly. "Let's find out all we can about Miss Emma. Such a lovely, dignified name, don't you think? Far grander than Fannie Mae." She pulled a face before tugging Margaret from the foyer and out the front door.

☙ ❧

The road to Dunbar was fifteen miles along windswept hills and bramble-framed stone walls. They took it slowly on account of Margaret's condition. A good tread of sleigh and carriage paths had patted down the snow nicely for a smooth, easy ride on the horses. Along the way Margaret told Fannie Mae what Jonas had discovered the day before. She debated whether or not to tell her all the details and then reasoned that Fannie Mae had been lied to long enough. The only way they were going to get to the root of all this was if they were open and honest with each other.

"Jonas is hoping the post-mortem can prove his theory," Margaret explained at the tail end of the story.

Fannie Mae listened intently the entire time Margaret had spoken and remained quiet for some time after she finished. Margaret began to think perhaps Fannie Mae hadn't understood what she had said, and didn't quite comprehend the severity of Jonas's initial findings.

"What does this mean?" Fannie Mae asked after long last. They were riding abreast with their eyes focused on the road ahead.

"It means Emma was murdered," Margaret answered. "Murdered and left to freeze in the snow."

Fannie Mae said nothing for the rest of the journey into town. They arrived forty-five minutes later with red cheeks and eager anticipation.

"Perhaps we should warm at the public house, grab a bite to eat before seeking clues about Emma," Fannie Mae suggested.

Margaret nodded, thankful for the suggestion. Her toes were the worst off of any other body part. Luckily, two seats nearest the hearth were vacated almost as soon as the women entered. Fannie Mae stopped the barmaid before she had a chance to walk by. "Do you have any soup or stew on?" she asked as Margaret shrugged off her cloak.

"Yes, of course," the barmaid said, glancing to Margaret. "Two servings, yes?"

Fannie Mae nodded. "And some hot cocoa?"

"Give me a moment, Emma Sweetie." The barmaid gave Fannie Mae a wink before slipping off into the kitchen.

"She seems nice," Margaret said, taking a seat the table.

Fannie Mae appeared ready to bounce. "I think she knows me—" She stopped herself. "Er... Emma, I mean." She took Margaret's cloak and hung it from a hook on the wall before taking off her own.

"Emma!"

Margaret looked up and saw a young man approaching Fannie Mae, his face stern.

"We told you not to come in here anymore." He nearly growled as he grabbed her upper arm, intent on pulling her to the front door.

Fannie Mae squared her body toward him and pulled her arm away. "Unhand me!" she said.

Margaret stood, expecting to assist her friend, but she needn't have bothered. In the instant Fannie Mae turned, the young man's face paled with embarrassment. There must have been something in her face or demeanour that told him she wasn't who he thought she was. Fannie Mae was rubbing her arm when Margaret came to her side. The man had drawn a quick retreat to the other side of the room, stealing an unsure glance back at them before ducking from the entry door.

"Who do you suppose that was?" Margaret asked.

"My brother," Fannie Mae said.

"You mean Emma's brother."

"That's what I said, isn't it?"

Margaret couldn't bring herself to agree. Fannie Mae had been acting very strangely that day. First, she had started calling her mother by her Christian name and ever since they had arrived in Dunbar she had been speaking as if she and Emma were the same person.

"Stay here, Margaret," she said suddenly. "I won't be but a minute." Without a coat Fannie Mae left the public house. Through the large windows at the front Margaret could trace her movements as she crossed the street calling out to Emma's brother.

The barmaid returned, plunking two deep clay bowls of soup on their rounded table. "Is Emma coming back?" she asked.

"My friend isn't Emma," Margaret said, a slight hesitation in her voice. Margaret stole a glance to the window and could just see Fannie Mae's outline through the condensation that had accumulated on the glass panes. "Her name is Fannie Mae."

"Is she and Emma related or something?"

"You could say they are related."

"Well, if she's anything like Emma, your friend won't

have any troubles filling her dance card in this town, that's for sure," the barmaid said with a chuckle. She set down two large mugs of hot cocoa with a peppermint stick in each. "House special," she said when Margaret spied the candy.

"Can you tell me something?" Margaret touched the woman's arm gently before she had a chance to walk away. "Does Emma come in here often?" she asked.

The woman held on to the tray with one handle and let it hang at her side. "Why do you ask?" she asked in all seriousness. "Are you her mother?"

Margaret chuckled slightly. "No, just a friend."

"Well, as I understand it, your girl lived all her life in this town and I ain't ever heard of her darkening these doors until four months ago."

"Why do you suppose that is?"

The barmaid looked about before bringing her gaze back to Margaret. "The story goes it's her parents. They'ze keeps their offspring on a mighty tight leash. Caused quite a stir when she were coming in here every day or two. Now she's just one of the regulars." She gave a shrug and moved to the unoccupied table next to Margaret's and started filling her tray with empty glasses.

Margaret pulled her hot cocoa toward her. "When was the last time she was here?"

The barmaid wasn't quick to answer. She eyed Margaret suspiciously and didn't pause her task.

"We haven't seen her in a little while," Margaret said cautiously. "We're somewhat worried about her."

A moment passed before the barmaid spoke. "Well, I guess it was night a'fore last," she said. "She came in for supper carrying a bag as if she were travelling somewhere. I only remember cuz I tripped over it once or twice."

"Did she say where she was going?"

"She only said something about finding her destiny. I didn't think much of it, to tell the truth," she said. "Young women always come in here mooning over this man or that one, talking about how they are destined to be together. I figured one of her sweethearts finally got around to asking for her hand. She probably eloped or something. Don't worry, Miss Emma'll turn up eventually."

The barmaid stood erect, her tray overflowing and balanced on one strong arm. "Eat your soup," she said. "It'll get cold before ye know it."

Seconds later Fannie Mae was back, bristling from the cold. "This looks delicious," she said, taking her seat. She stirred her peppermint stick in her cocoa and warmed her hands on the side of the mug.

Margaret waited but Fannie Mae seemed in no hurry to spill what she had found out. "So..." Margaret said, "How did it go?"

Suddenly, Fannie Mae burst forward with excitement. "He's invited us to their house. He said their mother would love to meet me." She reached over the table and grabbed Margaret's hand. "Isn't it exciting, Margaret?" She nearly squealed with delight.

"What did you tell him?" Margaret asked.

"It seems they all know Emma was adopted," she said. "I merely said I thought she was my sister."

"This will come as a shock to them."

Fannie Mae shrugged. "Perhaps, but what could be better than finding long-lost family?"

"I was talking about finding out about Emma. Their daughter is dead. It will not be a happy homecoming," Margaret cautioned, "not when we are the ones thrusting them into a period of deep mourning."

Chapter 13

Emma's family lived in a thatched roof house on the edge of town. Despite it being winter, Margaret could tell the front garden was a labour of love, adoringly tended with garden beds all along the fence both inside the gate and along the roadway. A small Christmas wreath with tartan bow hung from the wooden gate at the end of the walk and a matching one could be seen on the front door.

Margaret and Fannie Mae walked their horses up to the weather-worn wooden fence.

"I'm so nervous," Fannie Mae said, placing a hand over her stomach. " I can scarcely breathe. What if they don't like me?"

Margaret was almost certain they wouldn't. Once the family heard that their daughter was dead, she had no doubt Fannie Mae's presence would only deepen their sense of loss.

Emma's brother appeared at the door, closing it behind him. "I'll take them 'round back," he said, gesturing to the horses.

"Margaret, this is Edward," Fannie Mae said when he was directly in front of them. She handed him the reins of her horse and encouraged Margaret to do the same, nearly pulling the reins from Margaret's grasp. "Edward, this is my dear friend, Margaret."

Edward gave a quick nod but didn't meet Margaret's gaze.

"Mama is waiting for you inside," he said, his eyes cast down. He led the horses away and Fannie Mae turned to the gate. She paused momentarily and inhaled a steadying breath.

"This place... I feel as if Emma's mother is my mother," she said. She turned to Margaret. "Is that strange?"

To Margaret it was exceedingly strange, but Margaret wasn't a twin, and she hadn't been separated from her kin at birth. Perhaps if she and Peter were raised separately,

Margaret would have felt something similar, a familial bond forged in the womb rekindled once they found each other again. Margaret imagined the sensation would have been made all the more strange by the fact that Emma had passed away and Fannie Mae was left to feel the pain of it. The longing never satiated. An empty space never filled.

Fannie Mae gave the knocker three gentle raps before pinching the sides of her cheeks and checking the positioning of her hair.

The door swung open hurriedly, revealing a somewhat plump woman of short stature. Her smile was warm and her eyes bright as she took in her daughter's twin on her doorstep. "Fannie Mae!" She opened her arms wide and embraced Fannie Mae warmly. "Come in, come in!"

Together Fannie Mae and Margaret walked through the door. The house smelled of fresh baked bread and something else, something sweet, Margaret guessed.

"Edward told me you looked a spitting image of our Emma and now that I see you I must concur." Emma's mother stood back, examining Fannie Mae from head to toe. "Yes, yes," she said, "same hair, same eyes, everything. I apologize for the mix-up, my dear," she said, as the front door opened again and Edward walked in behind them. "My boy can be a little aggressive at times, can't you, Edward?"

Edward said nothing and merely skirted the three of them on the way to the kitchen.

"We understand," Fannie Mae said. "Don't we, Margaret?"

Margaret nodded, not necessarily out of agreement but more so in greeting.

"Well then, come in Fannie Mae, Margaret, come in. We go by the name Campbell but feel free to call me Caroline." She led them into a nearby parlour and gestured to the sofa. "Take a seat, ladies."

Fannie Mae took a seat, pressing out the creases in her dress and pulling back her shoulders. Margaret could tell her friend was nervous. When she sat next to her on the sofa, she discreetly folded her hand over Fannie Mae's and gave a gentle squeeze.

"I'm sorry to say Emma isn't here today to greet you as well," Caroline said, her demeanour bubbly and not in any way aware of the sad news they brought. "She'll be quite upset to find out she missed you."

Fannie Mae turned her gaze to Margaret, begging her to be the one who revealed what had brought them to Dunbar in the first place.

Before either of them could say anything Edward entered the room wheeling a tea cart toward them. There was a small plate of cookies set in among the cups and saucers, milk and sugar.

"Thank you, Edward," Caroline said, standing to pour tea. "Please fetch your brothers from upstairs." The look exchanged between mother and son was full of knowing, which pointed to something Margaret couldn't quite put her finger on. She watched as Edward crossed the room, never having met Margaret's or Fannie Mae's gaze.

"I have four children," Caroline said, smiling as she poured tea. "Edward is our oldest. I have two more boys besides. Emma is our only daughter."

"Forgive me for asking, but are all your children foundlings?" Margaret asked, clearing her throat slightly. She was starting to feel hot at the collar, her mind telling her this visit might end badly for all of them.

"Oh, no, only Emma." Caroline smiled as she handed Margaret a teacup and saucer. "My husband and I had been married for years without so much as a hint God would bless us with a child. Edward was a surprise. And I very much wanted a daughter so we contacted a lovely woman at Wendall Hall." Caroline stopped. "Do you know it?"

"Margaret and I work there," Fannie Mae said, accepting the teacup and saucer she offered.

Caroline seemed surprised at this. "Do you now? Well, then you know Mrs. Bane."

Fannie Mae nodded.

"Mrs. Bane spoke to us about twin girls and we had originally agreed to the pair—" Caroline stopped herself. "I'm sorry to talk about you, my dear, as if you weren't one of the twins yourself."

"No, I don't mind. We want to hear the story, don't we, Margaret?"

Margaret winced, but no one seemed to notice.

"We were more than happy to adopt both girls but when we arrived to bring you home, Mrs. Bane told us another couple had already filled out the adoption papers for you. We really had no choice," Caroline said, taking her seat. "We were just so overjoyed to be parents once more the truth of the matter truly didn't hit me until a few weeks later." Caroline reached over and placed her hand on Fannie Mae's. "I have thought on you countless times over the years, my dear," she said. "Is she well? Is she happy?" Caroline looked to Margaret but quickly turned her gaze.

A succession of footfalls thundered down the stairs as Edward returned with his siblings.

"The other boys came as a bit of a shock, to tell the truth," Caroline continued, raising her voice over the noise.

The three boys filed in through the door and stood at near attention. Edward looked not much older than Fannie Mae. The other two were much younger and they seemed in awe of Fannie Mae's resemblance to their sister.

"You've met Edward," Caroline said, gesturing with an upturned palm. "Then there's Stephen and James."

"I'm ten," Stephen said quickly.

"I'm ten—" James smacked his palm to his face. "I mean, I'm eight."

Everyone laughed at the gaff.

"Don't you boys look splendidly grown up," Fannie Mae said.

"Very dashing, I must say," Margaret added.

The two younger boys beamed with pride, reminding Margaret of two of her cousins back home, George and Hubert, who were only slightly younger. Edward, a fully grown man, looked less than pleased to be paraded about and expected to perform. He turned to his brothers and tried to usher them from the room.

"Are you going to be our sister now?" little James asked.

"Hush," Edward said, pulling at their shoulders to coax them from the room.

"I've always wanted another sister," James was heard saying in the hallway.

"She ain't our sister," Edward said gruffly.

"Jamie, perhaps we should ask Father Christmas to bring us another one," Stephen said, in a loud whisper as they stomped back up the stairs.

Caroline chuckled. "I don't suppose there's much chance in that," she said. Her gaze met Fannie Mae, whose expression had fallen. "Don't mind Edward," Caroline said. "He can be a little off-putting. He and Emma haven't always got on. And it only worsened four months ago."

"What happened four months ago?" Fannie Mae asked.

Caroline didn't answer right away. She seemed to take a breath and contemplate her words carefully. "Emma found out we had adopted her."

In unison Margaret and Fannie Mae drew in a breath.

"I just found out yesterday," Fannie Mae said.

"Did you? Is that what prompted you to come here? To seek Emma out?"

Fannie Mae turned to Margaret. She appeared unable or unwilling to break the sad news that had brought them to the Campbells' front door.

"Mrs. Campbell," Margaret began, putting down her teacup on the table in front of her. "We're afraid we have some rather horrid news." Margaret closed her eyes. "As we said before, we work at Wendall Hall, and yesterday morning we... well, that is to say, I discovered your daughter in a snowbank outside our side door." Margaret stopped herself, wishing she weren't required to continue. "She had died sometime in the night."

Caroline's teacup shook in her hand violently, sputtering tea out the sides. Fannie Mae moved quickly to pull the china from her grasp.

"We are so sorry for your loss," Fannie Mae said.

"No, no," Caroline said, refusing to admit the reality before her. "It can't be."

"I'm afraid it's true, Mrs. Campbell," Margaret said, wanting to run. It was a horrid task telling someone their loved one had died. A task Margaret never wanted to repeat.

A wail of pain escaped Mrs. Campbell first before she covered her face with both her hands. The noise must have alerted the attention of Edward. Seconds later he was at his mother's side. "What happened?" he demanded gruffly, as his mother clung to him.

"It's Emma," Fannie Mae started, suppressing her own tears. "She's had an accident."

"What sort of accident?" he pressed.

"She may have slipped and fallen," Fannie Mae said. Margaret noticed how she avoided her gaze as she spoke.

"Or it may be more than that," Margaret inserted. "The police are investigating."

"Investigating?" Edward's tone was hardened. "How come no one's come here? No one told us."

Margaret swallowed nervously. "It took us a while to identify her. As you can appreciate, your sister looks like my friend and we... well, we mistook her identity."

As Margaret spoke Edward's face turned to stone. She could not tell if he grieved or if he was angry.

"I want to see her," Caroline said, between sobs.

"Mother, that isn't wise."

"I want to see my child!"

"You'll have to arrange it with the Haddington police," Margaret said. "Once the investigation concludes, you'll be permitted to bury your daughter."

No one said anything for some time. The only sounds came from Mrs. Campbell, who wept into her handkerchief.

Fannie Mae looked to Margaret. "Perhaps we should go," she said.

"Mrs. Campbell, Edward, I will let Deputy Chief Kelly know you have been informed. Perhaps he can give you more information regarding their investigation," Margaret said following Fannie Mae's lead in standing. "In the meantime, if you have any more questions or concerns, you may speak with Fannie Mae or me at Wendall Hall. We will make ourselves available to you."

As Fannie Mae walked in front of Caroline and Edward, Caroline snatched her wrist. "Thank you for coming, my dear," she said between sniffles. "Please know you are welcome here anytime."

Fannie Mae's expression brightened a little bit at this. "Thank you, Mrs. Campbell."

"Please, call me Caroline."

Edward left his mother briefly to see them to the door. "Your horses are in the barn," he said.

When Margaret got to the hall she saw the faces of James and Stephen peering through the slats of the banister at them, most likely drawn by the commotion. "Are you going to tell Father?" one of the boys asked their brother.

"Yes, now get upstairs," Edward barked.

Neither of his brothers listened to him.

"I am so sorry for your loss," Margaret said, aware of how her words of condolence fell flat.

Edward said nothing. He opened the front door and gestured with his hands for them to leave. Overcome with emotion Fannie Mae left quickly. Before Margaret had a chance to step out the door Edward was closing it on her.

"Are they going to come back?" she heard one of the young boys ask.

"Let us hope not," was Edward's curt reply.

❧ ☙

The visit went as well as Margaret anticipated. Fannie Mae looked almost despondent as they walked the laneway to the back of the house to retrieve their horses.

"Oh, that was just awful," she said once they reached the barn. "I know it was the right thing to do but I wish it weren't me who had to do it." She ran her hand down Annabelle's mane, smoothing out the hair and reassuring the animal.

Margaret walked around the front of the animals and started to untie Annabelle's reins from the post. Something red in the otherwise brown-and-grey barn caught her attention. She saw a mound of fabric tucked beneath one of the workbenches. Leaving the reins tied, Margaret went toward it.

"What is it, Margaret?" Fannie Mae asked, coming to the front of the horses.

Kneeling down, Margaret pulled the cloth and found it was heavy, laden down with something. Another strong tug and the cloth broke free, sliding toward her. It was a carpetbag. She remembered the barmaid telling her Emma had come to the public house with a bag.

Margaret opened the clasp on the top. Inside she found a small picture frame, some books, and clothing. Margaret didn't have to dig in too far to realize the contents most likely belonged to a woman. The lace at one of the shirt collars was enough to tell Margaret that. On the inside cover of one of the books Margaret saw the name Emma Campbell scrolled in black ink.

Fannie Mae drew closer but before Margaret could say anything a sound came from just outside the door. Someone was there. Fannie Mae turned quickly and Margaret stood as Mr. Campbell walked through the barn doors. He was an average-sized man with a strong stance and hardened gaze. His surprise at finding them there deepened his scowl. "What are you doing in my barn?" he asked gruffly.

"Our apologies, sir," Fannie Mae said, quickly pulling at the knot that kept Annabelle tied to the post. "We only came to give your wife a message."

Margaret came to her feet and used her skirt to hide the carpetbag. Slowly, not wishing to make any noise, she pushed the bag with her feet back into its place beneath the workbench.

"What sort of message?" Mr. Campbell asked.

Fannie Mae looked to Margaret, who stepped forward to untie her horse.

"It's about Emma, sir," Margaret said. "I'm sorry to inform you but your daughter's body was found yesterday morning."

He gave them a quizzical look and glanced back at the house. "You told my wife this just now?"

"Yes. I'm so sorry for your loss," Margaret said, finally able to pull her horse free from the post.

Without another word he left them and hurried for the house.

"It doesn't feel right just to leave," Fannie Mae said.

"I'm afraid we must," Margaret said. "They must be left to their grief."

Fannie Mae led both her horse and Margaret's horse from the barn. Before Margaret left through the doorway she glanced back to where she knew the carpetbag hid. In the dust on the floor she should see lines where she had pulled it out, and hoped whoever was hiding it there didn't notice it had been disturbed.

Chapter 14

By the time they made it back to Wendall Hall it was mid-afternoon. The sun was warming the landscape enough to melt much of the snow from the roads, making their trek muddy and damp all the way from Dunbar. When they finally entered the carriage house, leading the horses in behind them, Margaret could sense Fannie Mae was in a foul mood. She hadn't said much during the entire journey, which was atypical for a woman like Fannie Mae.

With her horse safely deposited in an empty stall, Margaret scanned the inside of the building for signs of Benson and found him seated on a stool toward the back wall. His posture was slumped and his eyes downcast.

"Are you all right, Mr. Benson?" Margaret called out, as Fannie Mae clasped the stall door shut with their horses safely inside.

Margaret walked toward him.

"I'm all right, Mrs. Davies," he said, looking at her sideways and then quickly averting his gaze. A sniffle escaped him. "Just thinking," he said.

The back area of the carriage house was Benson's hideaway. It was where he kept his tools and projects. His cottage was somewhere else on the property, given to him by Violet as part of his contract of employment. Most of his time was spent in the carriage house tinkering. For an old man he was quite active, always on the move and showing no signs of slowing down.

As Margaret neared she could feel the aura of warmth radiating from a stout stove next to his workbench. This was his lifeblood throughout the winter months; without it, she was almost certain he'd freeze. Instinctively, she rubbed her hands together and inched them toward the stove. While warming up she saw a line of whittled animal forms, shaped from pine and aspen wood, lining a shelf. Some were painted but most were not. She also spied baskets of all types, some of willow but most of them woven with flat reeds in all variations of brown, hanging from the rafters, and nails hammered into the timber frame of the building. Margaret recognized some of the patterns and realized there were many similar baskets scattered throughout the hall. A line of willow baskets had prominent placement in the cloakroom. She had seen another set of large baskets in the kitchen. It suddenly struck her that two bassinets in the nursery looked to be another example of his handiwork. And every guest room had a basket of some sort, which up until then Margaret believed Violet had bought in town, never imagining it was Benson who had created them.

Margaret looked to Fannie Mae and discovered that she too was mesmerized by the treasure trove of handcrafted items.

When Benson lifted his gaze, Margaret saw that he had been crying.

"Are you thinking about Emma?" she asked, coming alongside him.

"Is that her name then?" Benson asked.

Behind her Margaret heard Fannie Mae touch something on one of the shelves. Looking over her shoulder, Margaret saw Fannie Mae handling a horse she had plucked from a nearby shelf. At first, Fannie Mae seemed curious and then her interest morphed into scrutiny as she drew the figure toward her for a closer look.

Suddenly, Benson was embarrassed and moved to cover up the carved animals closest to him with a hastily grabbed thin cloth.

"No, don't do that," Margaret said. "They are very good."

"Nah, this one's hind quarters are too long. And this one"—he pulled down a rabbit—"his ears are too short."

"I wouldn't even have noticed had you not pointed it out," Margaret said, trying not to look to Fannie Mae, who had returned the wooden horse to the shelf and was now scrutinizing a small basket.

"You are too kind, Mrs. Davies," he said, abandoning his attempt to hide his creations.

Margaret could not help but feel empathy for him. She had believed Fannie Mae when she said he was sour and unfriendly, deserving of their ridicule. Now she saw he was more likely just shy, ill at ease around people, and would prefer to work in the quiet of the carriage house among his creations than interact with those who were most likely to distrust him. Fannie Mae had been wrong about him, and Margaret had been wrong to believe her rather than judge for herself.

"That girl"—he lowered his voice—"have they discovered what done her in?" Benson finally asked. He ran a handkerchief under his nose and avoided her gaze.

"My husband thinks she suffered a blow to the back of the head," Margaret said.

"I should have tended the walk way better," he said. "I know how slippery it gets."

"No, it wasn't the ice or the snow," Margaret said. "Someone hit her."

"Hit her?" Benson pulled his shoulders back as if in shock. "Nah, ain't no one as callous as that."

Margaret was trying to think of what to say when Fannie Mae spoke from behind her.

"Where were you that night?" she asked, her expression like stone.

Benson was flustered by her question. "Here, of course, all evening."

Margaret spied a glass bottle behind a half-finished basket on one of the shelves. "Was this the gin?" she asked, reaching for it. It was a sizable bottle with only an inch of liquid left in the bottom.

Benson snatched it from her grasp and quickly hid it in a drawer behind him. "Yes," he said bluntly, snapping the drawer shut.

"May I see the bow?" she asked. Margaret scanned for the red bow Benson had spoken of and even looked in the waste bin.

"The what?" Benson asked, confused.

"The bow. You said you thought the bottle of gin was a present because of the bow," Margaret explained.

Benson did not move from in front of the drawer. "I threw it in the fire," he said.

"I wish you hadn't done that," Margaret said, closing her eyes and rubbing a hand over her forehead.

"What does it matter now?" Benson asked. "What do ye need the bow for?"

"What if it were a trick?" Margaret said. "A way to occupy you while someone gets away with murder? The bow, the fabric, the knot, it could tell us things about whoever gave it to you."

"That's not what happened," Benson said, clearly disturbed by the idea.

"But now we'll never know!" Fannie Mae said from behind Margaret.

Margaret raised her hand in an effort to calm Fannie Mae down.

"It didn't happen like that," Benson answered.

"How do you know?"

"Because there was no bow!"

Margaret and Fannie Mae both looked to Benson in surprise. All of a sudden, Benson realized what he had just said. "I lied, Mrs. Davies," he said, turning his back to them. "There was no bow." He offered an unsure glance to Fannie Mae and then focused his sights on Margaret, who was no doubt the more sympathetic of the two. "I was so upset after our argument about the horses, I came back here and found the bottle I had hidden in the rafters." Sheepishly, he pointed to the beams above them. "Ms. Violet is sure to sack me if she knew. That's why I lied. You ain't going to tell her, are ye?"

Margaret was slow to respond, unsure what the proper action might be, but before she could say anything Fannie Mae spoke from behind her.

"You lying weasel!"

"Fannie Mae!"

"It's true, Margaret, and you know it. Mother said he was never to be trusted. My only regret is not keeping my promise to stay clear of him."

"N-now, your mother... she is a f-fine woman," Benson said, stammering slightly as he spoke. "I ain't have nothin' but good things to say of her."

Fannie Mae narrowed her gaze. "How are you acquainted with my mother?"

"C-Church, 'course. I never said nothing to her, never in my life. N-never had reason to."

"You are always staring at her," Fannie Mae said, "I've seen it. It's the creepiest thing, Margaret."

"Mrs. Harris is pretty as a picture. Ain't nothing wrong with looking," he said, more to Margaret than Fannie Mae. "I-I don't know why she'd think badly of me, though. I ain't done nothing to Mrs. Harris, nor Miss Emma neither."

Margaret could sense Fannie Mae seething behind her, unwilling to accept Benson's innocuous reasoning. "Walk me through everything you did after you came back to the carriage house," Margaret said. "What did you do after you found the bottle?"

"I drank for a while—"

"How many glasses did you have?" Fannie Mae asked, accusatorily.

"I had no need of a glass," Benson said. "It's just as potent drank from the bottle."

"How barbaric."

Margaret winced at Fannie Mae's harsh words. "What did else did you do that night?"

"I-I went to my c-cottage."

"What time did you do that, Mr. Benson?"

"Around... midnight, I s'pose." He shifted uncomfortably on his stool. "After that I didn't set foot in Wendall Hall or near that side door." He leaned slightly to the side, as if to look around Margaret and direct his answer to Fannie Mae.

"It's all righ—"

"Did anyone see you?" Fannie Mae asked, cutting off Margaret's words.

"No..." He pulled up his shoulders in a shrug and appeared dumbfounded at what to say to defend himself.

"Fannie Mae, I think we need to exercise caution," Margaret said, turning. Her friend was standing with her arms crossed over her chest, and her eyes shot daggers at the man behind them.

"Benson's never done anything violent or threatening to any of us before." Margaret touched Fannie Mae's arm, attempting to comfort her, but Fannie Mae snapped it away.

"I'm beginning to question your loyalties, Margaret." Fannie Mae's gaze burned into her. It was a culmination of animosity gathered from all their disagreements that day. "My sister was murdered, you said so yourself. She was deliberately hit. Twice. That's what Dr. Davies said, wasn't it?"

"Yes, but we don't know by whom." Margaret was careful to keep her tone even. Throughout the day she had been sensing Fannie Mae's anger and righteousness growing, confidence intermingling with anxiety. "It's never a good idea to start pointing fingers at people until we gather as much evidence as we can."

As Margaret spoke, Fannie Mae grew more disgusted. She clearly was not interested in Margaret's even approach. Fannie Mae had found something worth fighting for, something that mattered to her, and she had no intention of letting any possible perpetrators go without proper interrogation.

"My mother is weeping because of the actions of that man—"

"Which mother exactly?" Margaret asked, her patience running thin. "The only mother you've been kind to the last twenty-four hours is a woman you just met."

"That's not fair!"

"It is fair," Margaret said, aware of her own frustration, "Mrs. Harris raised you. She chose you and loved you. She tended to you as an infant and nursed you when you were sick. You could try to show her some more appreciation."

"You heard Mrs. Campbell. She would have raised me and Emma together had Mr. and Mrs. Harris not snatched me up first. You haven't any idea how many times I begged Mother and Father for a brother or sister, and all this time I've had a twin just a few miles down the road."

Most children beg for a sibling at one point or another. Margaret herself could remember asking her mother for a sister, and just as quickly saying 'If it's another boy we shall send it back.' At five she hadn't any real idea how siblings came to be. Fannie Mae didn't seem to realize how common her wish had been among other children.

"I knew something was missing from my life," Fannie Mae continued. "Emma was missing and *that man* took her away from me forever. He thought she was me and decided to murder me!"

Behind her Margaret heard the sounds of weeping, the choked breathing and sniffling that accompanied deep and painful emotions. Coming to a stand, Benson began to stammer, his intended words lost among the shallow breaths and shaking of his jaw. "For the last time...I did not hurt that girl!" He plucked up the stool he had been sitting on and, with great force and frustration, hurled it at the wall behind him.

Margaret and Fannie Mae recoiled in fright as the wooden object splintered into a handful of pieces.

"Do you see, Margaret?" Fannie Mae said once their shock subsided. "That man is more than capable!" She pulled a sickened face and met Margaret's gaze. "When he's heading for the gallows I will remember how you defended him and I shall never forgive you for it." With that, Fannie Mae turned on her heels and marched for the door.

☙ ❧

Benson repeated numerous apologies as they worked to clean up the mess of wood, throwing the bits and pieces in the lit stove. "I ain't done nothing wrong, Mrs. Davies," he said between sniffles. "Please say you believe me."

Margaret couldn't say exactly why but she did indeed believe him. "Don't worry, Mr. Benson," she said. "Everything will come out all right in the end." Her words, though welcome, did not entirely appease his worry. She only left him once she knew he was alright.

She hesitated to use the side door and the walkway where Emma's body was found, even though it now looked as if nothing untoward had ever taken place there. With marked determination, Margaret headed down the path, her gaze up and her thoughts distracted from the difficult reality she faced. Opening the door, she instantly regretted her decision. Deputy Chief Kelly was standing on the other side. He had turned at the sound of the door and regarded her strangely as she entered. "Mrs. Davies," he said.

"Mr. Kelly." She nodded in acknowledgment and moved to pass him but his attention followed her.

"Your husband gained access to my body yesterday," he said.

Margaret gave a closed-mouth smile. "Professional curiosity, I suppose," she said.

Deputy Chief Kelly appeared amused at this. "I highly

doubt it."

Knowing whatever she said in response would be regarded as either suspicious or condescending, Margaret turned and walked away. Partway down the hall her conscience forced her to stop.

"Mr. Kelly, you should know that I have discovered the identity of the woman," she said, finally committing to what she knew she must do. "I believe her name is Emma Campbell of Dunbar."

"Is that so?"

"Yes." Margaret wanted to pull her gaze away from his hardened glare but knew doing so would only imply a degree of guilt. "Turns out, Miss Campbell is indeed Fannie Mae Harris's twin sister, separated at birth,"

Deputy Chief Kelly's mouth dropped half an inch in surprise. He stammered but was unable to form the words of a thousand questions that must have been running through his mind.

Margaret took a step forward, careful to keep her voice low. "Miss Harris had not realized she was a twin, nor did she know she was a foundling for that matter, until we spoke with her mother yesterday. As you can imagine, this has all come as a great shock to not only Miss Harris but all of us." She waited a few seconds, inviting him to say something but he remained silent. "We went to Dunbar today to see the Campbells—"

"You went to see them?"

Margaret blanched. "Well, yes. I needed to confirm my suspicions and, turns out, I was correct."

"Your suspicions..." Deputy Chief Kelly moved toward her. "How did your suspicions first formulate? Who is feeding you this information?"

Margaret hesitated. She resisted the urge to look to the nursery door. She still wasn't sure of Kelly's character and the least amount of people caught in his investigative snare the better. "I overheard a conversation," she said, raising her chin a degree. "Emma Campbell had been here a week ago. She had a meeting with Mrs. Bane."

"Is that so?" His words were dragged out, menacing and almost delighted.

"I only tell you this to assist the direction of your

inquiries," she explained. "I do not believe Violet Bane is involved in any manner."

"That remains to be seen, Mrs. Davies."

Margaret knew his words to be true. Any number of her coworkers could be caught up in this tragedy. The only thing she knew for sure was that she and Jonas were not responsible in any way.

"Your evidence leads me to my next question, Mrs. Davies: why did Emma Campbell travel here a week ago and what brought her back the other night?"

"I don't know, sir," Margaret said. "That is just something you, yourself, are going to have to find out."

"Am I to believe your intention is to allow the actual investigators to investigate?" he asked, his tone somewhat mocking.

"If that is what you actually do," she said. "By all means, investigate."

He smiled at this but Margaret did not wish to wait to see if he had anything else to say to her. She ducked into the door that led to the kitchen and nearly ran into Violet.

"Oh, Margaret, I'm so glad you are here." She hesitated as if wanting to say more but restrained herself. "The detective is back and wishes to meet with me. Can you bring some extra blankets to Miss Brundell in Room 207, and perform a quick exam? I've been so busy with all this business, I'm afraid she feels neglected."

Margaret didn't bother hiding her fear. "Oh please, I can't, not Miss Brundell—"

"Margaret, please. I've spent all day interviewing adoptive parents and haven't spent one minute with the patients." Violet walked in a circle, skirting Margaret until finally she was at the door to the hallway. "I'd very much like to talk with you at some point," she said, an apology in her tone. She looked at Margaret expectantly. "I haven't the time at present but"—she reached out and squeezed Margaret's upper arm—"promise me you won't make any rash decisions, not before hearing what I have to say."

Absentmindedly, Margaret nodded. While she should have been focusing on Violet's words, all she could think about was having to face her friend from London, the one who'd ignored her greeting just the day before.

In the hallway outside Bethany's room, Margaret decided she would act as she would with any of the patients at Wendall Hall. She envisioned herself walking in through the door, smiling, without any hint that the two women had a prior affection for one another. The exercise made Margaret feel more homesick than she already was. Nothing would ever be the same.

After taking a deep breath, Margaret squared her shoulders, curled the edges of her mouth into a smile, and rapped gently on the door.

"Yes?"

Margaret pushed in. "I've come with more blankets," Margaret said, careful to keep her voice light.

Bethany was standing at the window, her arms crossed over her chest. There was no one else in the room with her. Once she realized who it was Bethany rushed for the door and closed it, urging Margaret to come farther into the room. "Oh, Margaret!" she exclaimed in a hushed tone. "I'm so glad you are here."

Margaret didn't know what to make of it. She moved where Bethany guided her but she remained dumbfounded, hugging the folded blankets to her chest.

"Aunt Jane has finally left me for Edinburgh. She wished to visit friends while I…" Bethany's voice trailed off as she drew Margaret's attention to her very pregnant mound at her midsection. "Oh, look at the mess I find myself in." She grabbed Margaret's arm and pulled her toward the bed like she used to do when she had some salacious gossip to exchange. "You had no idea, did you, the last time we saw each other?"

Margaret shook her head as Bethany took a seat on the edge of the bed. "I had no idea. Why didn't you tell me?"

"Oh, I couldn't!" Bethany looked genuinely horrified at the thought. "I could barely admit my predicament to myself."

"But I could have helped you," Margaret said, placing the folded blankets down on the foot of the bed.

Bethany shook her head, resigned to her present state of

111

affairs. "No, darling Margaret," she said, "this is my burden, not yours."

"But what about the father? Surely he must account for his actions."

Bethany chuckled. "If all men faced their responsibilities do you believe a place like Wendall Hall would need to exist?" She shook her head. "The father of this child has left to seek his fortunes in America, which is just as well, as I was beginning to tire of his moody rants against the establishment."

"Goodness, Bethany, imagine you falling for a radical!"

"Oh, I wouldn't call it falling, more like clumsily tripping. I swear, the predicaments I get myself into." She ran her open palm over the crest of her stomach as she looked down. "No one knows," she said. "Not even Mother and Father. Aunt Jane had only sussed it out of me three months ago and she made arrangements for us to 'travel the continent'. I am under strict orders to have this baby now so we can return for Christmas."

Margaret looked at her sympathetically. "Babies have their own timing." She took in the sight of her dear friend, and was thankful their friendship hadn't been tarnished for the long term. "I'm sorry about yesterday," she said. "I'm still getting used to my role here. Violet warned me when I started that I may encounter some people I knew. I guess I just never really thought about it actually happening. We are so far removed from London. It's so remote up here."

Bethany's eyes widened as she nodded. "Yes! I don't know how you stand it. But I suppose newlyweds don't need many diversions, not in the first year anyway."

Margaret blushed. "I am sick for home," she admitted. "I haven't seen Peter or Aunt Louisa in months. Or the boys. Not since Father died."

"That was a tragic business, Margaret. His impairment and all." Bethany tsk-tsk'd and shook her head. "I'm sorry I didn't come. I've been a little occupied."

And so their reunion went for another hour, chatting as if no time had passed since their last cup of tea together, as if their affection for each other had not waned in the slightest.

Chapter 15

Margaret was in the kitchen when Maisie appeared in the doorway. Dressed for travel, she clutched a small carpetbag in front of her with both hands. "Ms. Violet said you are able to escort me to the train station," she said, her words hesitant and unsure. "She said you'd be heading home for the day and could see me to the village." Her slight figure still looked weak from childbirth and her features bore the pain of having given up her child.

"Yes of course, but"—Margaret glanced at the kitchen maid who was busy making her a tea—"do you think you are ready for travel?"

"I really haven't a choice," Maisie answered. She tilted her chin slightly and that's when Margaret saw evidence that she had been crying.

"Perhaps you'd like a hot tea before we go," Margaret offered.

"If it's all the same to you, Ms. Margaret, I'd like to go now, while my strength is willing."

Margaret could not help but feel a palpable sadness wash over her. Maisie had been there for over a week and had been the first birth mother who she coached completely on her own. "Of course," she said. "Let me fetch my coat and we shall have Benson hitch the carriage."

Within half an hour, they were on the road heading for Helmsworth. Maisie sat quiet for a long time, and only spoke when the two churches in the village square came into view.

"Helmsworth seems like such a delightful town," Maisie said. "It's the sort of town you read about in novels."

Margaret smiled. "Yes, I suppose it is."

"I'll never get the chance to live in a town such as this," Maisie said.

"Oh, you never know." Margaret would never have guessed such a change for herself. Growing up she'd always imagined a marriage and lifestyle more resembling the one of her parents, loveless and extravagant.

A slight chuckle escaped Maisie. "No, I do know. Girls like me don't end up in places like this. Them that washes and cooks from sunup to sundown don't often get to visit a place like this, let alone live here."

The train was already at the station. As soon as Benson pulled up the carriage to the platform steps Maisie and Margaret sprang out and headed for the ticket counter.

"One ticket to Edinburgh, please," Margaret said, pulling some change from her pocket.

Maisie smiled when Margaret turned to her and handed her the ticket. "I'm going to miss you, Ms. Margaret," she said, slipping the ticket into her carpetbag. "I knew you were kind-hearted the moment I saw you."

Maisie's compliment warmed Margaret's heart and then unwillingly her mind went to Fannie Mae, who no longer held Margaret in such high regard.

The train whistle blew, loud and robust.

"Take care of yourself, Maisie," Margaret said, walking with her to the steps that would take her aboard one of the train cars. "Remember what Mrs. Bane taught you. You do not want to find yourself in this position again anytime soon."

"Yes, ma'am," Maisie replied. Before she climbed the step she leaned into Margaret for an embrace. "I'd invite you to tea but..."

Margaret nodded. Once Maisie stepped on that train, their connection would be over. Even if Margaret saw her on the street she'd not be permitted to call out to her.

"And I hope you find out who was behind that sad business at the Hall," Maisie said. "Doesn't seem right ... I should have said something."

"It's not your fault," Margaret said.

"I've been thinking about it since we spoke..." Maisie said, yelling over the sound of the compressed air seeping through the vents below the car. "I think there was an argument. I thought it was voices from inside the building but now I'm not so sure."

"Was it outside?" Margaret yelled, inching closer so they could hear each other.

Maisie nodded. "And I don't think it was—"

The locomotive whistle blew, drowning out Maisie's words. She cupped her free hand around her mouth, as if knowing Margaret was having trouble hearing her.

"ALL ABOARD!"

"I can't hear you!" Margaret shouted.

The train conductor came between them urging Margaret to step back from the train and then directed Maisie inside. Flustered, Maisie scrambled awkwardly inside the train car for an available seat, waving through the windows for Margaret to follow her down the platform. Once seated, Maisie blew warm breath on the cold glass. Margaret watched mesmerized as Maisie used her finger to draw lines and soon Margaret realized she was trying to spell out something.

NAMTOON

Namtoon? The word made no sense.

Margaret remembered Maisie didn't have much education. It was said, in many upper circles, that the best servants were illiterate ones. Though Margaret herself didn't believe in such things, she knew many other more established households still held on to the adage. She'd have to ponder Maisie's final word to her and hoped to decipher it later on.

Despite her confusion, Margaret nodded anyway and Maisie quickly used her sleeve to erase what she had written. As the train inched down the line the women waved their final goodbyes before Maisie forced herself to look away. Margaret saw her brush away a tear before Maisie was obscured from her view.

Once the end of the train had rolled away from the platform and wound its way around the bend, Margaret turned, the finality of her connection with Maisie hitting her harder than she expected. Two days ago they had bonded over one of life's most precious moments and now it was over and they'd most likely never see each other again. What was to stop her from thinking on Maisie years from then, or any of the other girls she had helped while working at Wendall Hall? How does Violet do it? How does she provide such intimate care to a nearly steady stream of women and their babies and not somehow feel a lingering connection to every one of them?

Margaret was alone on the platform and took a fright when she saw two sets of eyes peering from around the depot building. Two sets of eyes from a pair of very curious little boys. Once they realized they had been spotted, they ducked back behind the cover of the wall. With silent footfalls, Margaret inched toward the edge of the building. Turning the corner, she saw Stephen and James at the bottom of the steps.

"You say something," James hissed, elbowing his brother forward.

Stephen said nothing and nudged his brother back, neither of them realizing Margaret was right there.

"Say something about what exactly?" Margaret asked.

They gasped in near unison and their eyes grew wide at the sight of Margaret. Their feet shuffled on the gravel beneath them. "We were standing over there by the fence when we saw you," James said, gesturing to the butcher shop, not too far from the train depot.

"You came to the house," Stephen said quickly.

"She knows that, dummy," James said.

"When you left Mama was crying," Stephen explained, his eyes watching Margaret closely as she walked down the steps to be level with them.

"I didn't mean to make her cry," Margaret said. "Someone else did a very bad thing."

"They hurt Emma," James said. "Edward told us."

Margaret winced internally. The boys were far too young to be experiencing such things. They had lost their sister. And Margaret had no doubt that it would haunt them forever.

"Did a policeman come to your house this afternoon?" Margaret asked, wondering if Kelly would respond so quickly to the information she gave him.

"Oh yes," James answered. "He talked with Papa and Mama for a very long time."

"A very, very long time," Stephen emphasized.

"Mama didn't want to let us leave the house," James explained. "But we begged Papa to bring us along."

Margaret followed their gaze to the butcher's. Mr. Campbell appeared at the front door, his arms laden with a wooden crate of sundries. Just the appearance of him seemed to set the boys on edge.

"We have to go, ma'am," James said, grabbing Stephen's hand and pulling him in the direction of their father.

Margaret followed. "I should like to ask him a few questions," she said, picking up her pace as they crossed the road. Little Stephen fought his brother's grip with every step. He had twisted his body so he could face Margaret but James would not let go.

Mr. Campbell stopped at the walk and offered a hardened scowl as the boys approached. When his eyes lifted to Margaret, they did not change. For a moment she wondered if his frustration had deepened at the sight of her.

"Take this," he said, turning the box over to the boys. "Between the both of you now. It's heavy."

Without hesitation the boys accepted the box and, although they struggled with the heavy burden, they performed their task with only the smallest of grunts and no complaints, walking sideways farther along the walk to their carriage.

"What is it?" he asked Margaret gruffly. "Have you come to bring news of another loved one of mine found dead?"

"No," Margaret answered, a little surprised by his forthright resentment toward her. "Believe me when I say I wish we could have met under better circumstances."

He grunted and started to walk away, disinclined to converse with Margaret longer than absolutely necessary.

"Mr. Campbell, sir, my name is Margaret Davies. I've just moved here with my husband, Dr. Davies, and unfortunately I never had the chance to meet your daughter."

He eyed her but did not slow his pace.

"I am so sorry for your loss."

"I don't wish to talk about it."

"But, sir, I just have a few questions, if I may. Miss Harris is very anxious to learn all she can about her twin sister." Margaret hurried ahead of him, forcing him to look at her.

He stopped short of colliding with her.

"What does it matter now?" he asked. "She's gone. She isn't anyone's sister any longer." He moved as if to brush past her but Margaret shifted slightly to bar his way and stood her ground.

"It may not matter to you but, I assure you, to Miss Harris it means a great deal." She saw his shoulders slump and though he said nothing Margaret understood it as permission to continue. "We are afraid something malicious may have been carried out on Emma." She glanced farther down the road to ensure Stephen and James were outside of hearing distance. "We believe she may have been attacked."

"What do you mean 'we'?" he asked.

"My husband and I. He's a surgeon with the medical school at the university. He's been assisting with the case, to help find answers."

The fact that Jonas had not been actively asked for input or that both he and Margaret were not involved directly with the police investigation did not pass her lips. Of course any information she'd discover she'd pass on to Deputy Chief Kelly but she had a feeling that as a civilian, a woman to boot, that she'd experience far more luck at getting answers than a stodgy officer of the law in a dark blue uniform.

"We believe she may have been murdered, that the intent was to harm and perhaps even kill Emma." Margaret watched him closely. "I have to ask if there is anyone whom you might be aware of who would wish your daughter harm?"

Mr. Campbell appeared unaffected by news that his daughter might have been murdered and seemed more concerned with the embarrassing way their private lives had been laid bare. "My daughter was a challenge for her mother and me. I am quite certain she would have been a challenge for many others in her life."

"She was a challenge in what way?" Margaret asked.

"Insolent. Brooding. Only ever looking for ways to disobey us." He let out a breath, and was unable to look Margaret in the eye. "She wasn't always like that, mind you," he said. "She had always been a good-natured girl. She was helpful with the boys and her mother. I think I should like to remember her that way."

"When did her behaviour change exactly?" Margaret

asked.

"Four months ago," he said. He hesitated before saying more. "She found out about the adoption. We didn't tell her willingly. After that she was just different. If she didn't come home we knew she was at the public house. Caroline suspected a young man, but..." His voice trailed off. He took a deep breath and rubbed at the back of his neck.

"Mr. Campbell, I hope you won't mind me asking, but do you suspect your daughter may have been in the family way?" Margaret asked. "Is that why she was coming to Wendall Hall?"

Mr. Campbell scoffed at her. "How well does a father know these things?" He regarded her harshly and then shifted his gaze just over her shoulder. "If that were the case she's better off dead, in my opinion. Better than bringing disgrace to all of us like that." His eyes found her again, but this time they bore into her, a hardened stare meant to intimidate and instill fear.

In that instant, Margaret's throat went dry.

"She's gone, Mrs. Davies, and there ain't nothing the police, or you, can do to change that fact. I'll thank you to say nothing more about little Emma's secret. I don't know what kind of woman you are, but I'll remind you that you don't know the kind of man I am." He pushed forward, sliding between Margaret and the hedge and walking quickly toward the carriage where James and Stephen waited.

Chapter 16

"Mrs. Davies!" Annalise's voice betrayed her surprise as she stood in the foyer, one arm in her coat in an awkward fashion. Margaret had just pushed open the door and was surprised to find her maid-of-all-work leaving for the day. The pair danced awkwardly, trading places in the narrow space between the front door, the stairway, and the hall to the rest of the house.

"I've put a roast chicken in the oven," Annalise said, quickening her pace once Margaret no longer barred her path to the door. "It should be ready in the hour."

Margaret nodded thankfully and watched as the maid hurried to leave. "Oh, Annalise, have you ever heard the word 'namtoom' before?" she asked, hoping it was a local word, perhaps even a bit of the Scots Gaelic from years past.

If it was, however, Annalise had never heard of it. She shrugged with a pronounced look of confusion.

"Thanks all the same," Margaret said, before her eyes found the small envelope positioned on the hall table at the base of the stairs. In dark pen was scrolled 'Dr. & Mrs. Davies'.

"What's this?" Margaret asked. As soon as she said it she recognized Annalise's handwriting and knew it must have been a letter from her.

By the time Margaret opened the unsealed flap of the envelope, Annalise was buttoning the last of the buttons on her coat. "I cannot manage it another moment," she said rather quickly, seeming desperate to be out the door and on her way. It was clear Annalise hadn't intended Margaret to be there when she left. "I cannot work for a man and wife so strange and peculiar."

Margaret nearly laughed. "Peculiar how?" When she looked Margaret saw the young woman was ill amused. Annalise raised her chin and tightened her jaw in response.

"I cannot, in good conscious, align myself with a woman

who would... who would... involve herself with such scandal." The strength of her conviction appeared lost once Margaret directly questioned her. Once she started speaking, her words, which began as direct and loud, softened and she appeared unsure.

"Annalise, you knew I had a position at Wendall Hall before you started with us. I was very clear to all the applicants so that there would be no misunderstanding."

"That was before," Annalise said.

"Before what exactly? The murder?"

Annalise looked disinclined to answer directly. Even as she stood at the door, her notice of resignation written and in Margaret's hand, Margaret wondered if she truly meant to give up her place.

"I am merely helping the investigation," Margaret said. "You must understand, these types of inquiries come as naturally to me now as breathing."

"Wives and mothers-to-be do not associate themselves with such things," Annalise said. "Married women don't work and they don't mistake themselves for detectives."

"What else do you expect me to do? I would sooner shave my head and join a monastery than sit at home tatting lace doilies all day."

The maid's eyes widened at Margaret's words.

"You cannot expect me to be anything other than what I am," Margaret continued. "And I thank the heavens my husband does not share your constraining views."

Margaret had no doubt that if Jonas expected her to change after marriage, to tend to the household to the detriment of everything else that made Margaret the woman she was, well, then she'd never have married him. Thankfully, aside from expressing concerns regarding her condition, Jonas let her do as she pleased and things were boding well for a long and happy marriage.

Annalise stood quiet at the door as Margaret finally pulled out the short note of resignation. Nothing of her reasoning was noted. After reading it, Margaret tossed it back to the table.

"If you feel so strongly that you must go, then go," Margaret said. "But I will say I am disappointed you would leave me so suddenly and only a few days before Christmas as well—"

"I'm sorry," Annalise said, her tone changed. "My husband has directed me to give notice," she said, giving the true reason at last. "He is unwilling to have me work for someone so modern. He thinks you will put ideas into my head. It's the same reason he would not let me take a place at Wendall Hall even though the pay is better and the work steady."

As she spoke Margaret could see the early stages of tears in the woman's eyes.

"He said women like you and Mrs. Bane teach women that men aren't needed."

"That's ludicrous," Margaret said, under her breath. "He's a coward if he thinks women who are given choices will mean the end of men," she said more directly, crossing her arms over her chest. "And anyone who agrees with him is a coward too."

"I am not a coward, Mrs. Davies, but I am a mother of three and my children and I are solely dependent upon him. I haven't the luxury of choice, not as you have, and that's the truth of it. I'm sorry, Mrs. Davies, but I must go." With that, Annalise turned and placed her hand on the doorknob. She hesitated briefly before pulling the door toward her and stepping out into the cold.

 ༄ ༅

By the time Jonas came home, Margaret had been seated at the kitchen table for over an hour poring over the copious notes she had taken while a dear friend, Mrs. Crane in Edinburgh, had showed her the very basics of cooking. The lessons had taken place weeks ago, shortly before Margaret and Jonas had moved to Helmsworth. While Margaret had every intention of teaching herself from them, after Annalise was hired she had become lax in her efforts. She was no closer to becoming a housewife than she had been when they first arrived at their cottage.

"What's this?" Jonas asked, after kissing Margaret on the forehead. He picked up one of the pieces of papers from the table and brought it closer to him.

"I'm looking for the one where Mrs. Crane taught me

about cooking fowl," she said. "I can't find it." When she looked up she found him looking at her peculiarly. "I'm going to make a goose for Christmas dinner," she said. "A small one, I think."

"Have you informed the butcher so he may make sure he has one? Even a *small* one?"

"The butcher?"

"Yes. You can be assured it will need to be arranged ahead of time."

Margaret blanched and dropped the paper in her hand. "Clearly, I haven't a clue what I am doing," she said as she rubbed her eyes.

"Oh come now." Jonas came to her side and pulled her into her arms, hugging her from behind.

"Why did no one ever teach me these things?" she asked, holding on to her husband's arm as he embraced her. "Why is it convention for some to toil while others are permitted to remain useless?"

"Goodness." Jonas pulled away and took a seat next to her so he could look her in the eyes. "What's brought this about?"

Margaret didn't want to tell him. She was afraid of alarming him. Imagine her seeing to all the household chores, simple tasks she wasn't remotely aware of how to do. He'd no longer have a freshly pressed shirt or a well-prepared meal. She hadn't the first clue how to clean, let alone how often to clean. When Annalise worked there she could at least pretend she was making progress but now it was clear she knew very little.

"Annalise submitted her resignation today," Margaret said. "She said her husband no longer wanted her working for such a modern couple. Well, actually she said strange and peculiar couple but then she said I was too modern a woman."

"That explains it," Jonas said.

Margaret wasn't entirely sure what he meant by that.

"Come now, Margaret, you must admit we are rather strange and peculiar." He offered a broad, playful smile.

She nudged him and tried to hide a smile of her own. "Sometimes I feel like I am turning into my mother more and more every day."

Jonas gave her a startled look.

"Not in that sense," she corrected herself, referring to her mother's lover, "but certainly in a social sense. She was regarded in a very similar way. Too good for certain company. Not good enough for others. It's as if we expect everyone to fit seamlessly into very specific categories. I do believe my mother was born before her time. She never let me believe I was restricted by anything. She let me and Peter be free to do as we chose. It was Father who expected us to behave as others would have us behave. When I think on it now, Mother encouraged me to spread my wings beyond my cage. I doubt Peter or I would have ever considered medical school had she not been there."

"Are you still considering medical school, given"—he nodded toward her round stomach—"your current condition?"

"I don't have much of a choice now, do I?" she said. "I might have been able to convince them to admit me as a single woman, but certainly not as a wife and young mother. Each day that goes by that reality becomes more and more apparent, I'm afraid." Margaret pushed herself up from her chair and circled the table, cleaning up her loose papers as she went.

"You're not displeased with me, are you?" Jonas asked.

"No, of course not, why would I be? You did not plan this any more than I did." She hated referring to their child as a hindrance rather than a blessing. While her condition demanded a quick marriage, she was well situated and hadn't been without options. She chose to be with Jonas, and she knew he had chosen to be with her. It was something they both decided to weather together; however, it affected their future.

"I only ask because you seem sullen lately," Jonas said, "and it's not just because of what happened at the Hall."

"I'm merely homesick, that's all," Margaret said. "Especially so close to the holidays." She could sense him studying her as she cleaned up her mess of papers. "I'm still adjusting to life as a wife, and soon I'll have to adjust to duties as a mother. I think any woman would find the transition challenging."

"But you are not regretful, for having to leave London

and your family?"

"No." Margaret shook off her husband's concern and inched toward him. "Everything will be all right in the end," she said, watching him stand and come toward her. "I just need to figure out a few things, most importantly how to keep us from starving."

Jonas laughed. "I don't believe there is much chance of that." He pulled her close, planting a kiss on the top of her head. Suddenly, he froze, lifting his nose higher in the hair. "What's that smell?"

When Margaret pulled her face from his chest she noticed smoke wafting into the air around them. She gasped. "The chicken!"

Chapter 17

Margaret felt even less chipper in the morning. Without Annalise there to help her she fumbled through her usual morning chores, which included washing up from breakfast and readying herself for work. Somehow she managed to arrange her hair and squeeze into her stays but as she walked the short distance from her home to the village square to meet Arthur she could not help but feel self-conscious, unequal to the Margaret of the day before. She thought she saw hesitation in Arthur's eyes the moment he lifted his gaze from the horses. She believed she looked a fright, and now, despite Arthur's attempts to pretend not to notice, she knew she did.

"Good morning, Mrs. Davies," he said, clearing his throat. She wondered if beneath his sing-song tone he questioned her morning's efforts, perhaps wondering what had happened to affect such a change in her appearance.

Things were more difficult when all alone, especially with a large round belly protruding out her front. Margaret's hand went up to the curls at her neck. Her pins had stayed, thank goodness, and her hair remained neatly tucked under her winter bonnet, but she felt awkward nonetheless. Perhaps she didn't look as disheveled as she thought she did. Perhaps it was all a matter of perspective.

"Good morning, Arthur," she said, taking his hand and using it to balance herself as she climbed into the sleigh. To Margaret's surprise he forewent with their usual morning commuting banter. His mind seemed far too occupied with other matters to dally in jests pertaining to Margaret's destination. They both knew where she was headed and it appeared like neither of them were in much of a mood to play around as they had before.

"Forgive me, Mrs. Davies," he said, as they cleared the village proper and started their journey along one of the country roads, "I'm guessing I'm a rather dull companion this morning."

"I don't mind," Margaret said in earnest. "I'm afraid I'm not much like myself today either."

"Such a sad business this," he said. "I heard tell it were you who found the body out there on the estate. I imagine it were a sight anyone would find disturbing, much less a refined woman like yourself."

In truth, it wasn't something Margaret had thought much about in the last two days; at least she hadn't thought about her feelings at any rate. She had allowed her work and the line of inquiry to consume her thoughts. The sight of the body in the snow had been quite disturbing, especially so when Margaret had believed it was her friend. Even though Fannie Mae was found alive, the notion that someone her own age could be struck down without warning and seemingly without cause was enough to give anyone, including Margaret, a reason to pause.

What exactly had Emma Campbell done to deserve such a violent end? How had her actions brought about such vengeful wrath? Perhaps her death had nothing to do with her actions. Perhaps she died at the hands of a wicked individual, someone who would have killed anyone given a proper chance. Margaret shivered at the thought of it. Such a scenario was highly unlikely. Murders were most often committed for a reason, though not always sound. There was usually a connection between the victim and the perpetrator. This is where Margaret needed to focus her attention. Determine the motive, Margaret told herself, and it will lead you to the killer.

"How is Mrs. Bane handling everything?" Arthur asked after a few minutes of driving in silence. "Is she managing?"

Margaret hadn't spoken with Violet much in the preceding twenty-four hours. She couldn't rightly say how Violet was faring. She suddenly felt abashed for not having spoken to her the day before, for allowing a few words said in frustration and haste to colour what had otherwise been an amiable partnership. In that moment, standing across the hall, Violet's dismissive words against Margaret's truest efforts ringing in her ears, Margaret had felt betrayed. A bored socialite she may be but why shouldn't she occupy her time with more meaningful work than embroidering pillows and practicing piano?

It seemed silly to expect women, once pregnant, to fade from public or any sort of pursuit to pass the time. What was Margaret doing after all than merely incubating the beginnings of a life? Put in plain words, it seemed glorious enough on its own, but the reality was that pregnancy, nine months of it, was a long process of minute growth. Her stomach ballooned without any assistance from Margaret. Aside from a slight adjustment of balance, and of course the earlier sickness which in and of itself was quite short-lived, thank goodness, Margaret felt no difference. She knew the worst was yet to come. Closer to her time, she knew her ankles would swell, her chest would burn, and her stomach would grow so large and weighted she would most definitely find it difficult to move about. But for the time being, there wasn't a whole lot she could do to move the pregnancy along or even ensure a healthy child. As she had said to countless women at Wendall Hall, her body knew what to do and it would do it. She merely had to withstand the discomfort of it while it took place.

It was for those reasons, and more besides, that Margaret took a place at Wendall Hall. Violet's misjudgments of her had been painful, yes, but more to that, she had revealed Margaret as a socialite, a woman of means, something Margaret had been actively trying to hide from her new incarnation as a doctor's wife and nothing more. She had been on a mission to reinvent herself, so to speak, and Violet had exposed her to the people she held dear, revealing her deception.

Margaret closed her eyes and bowed her head. "She's experiencing some difficulty, I'm afraid," Margaret said, realizing Violet had only behaved so because of the extraordinary amount of pressure she must be experiencing.

"Are the police behaving like brutes?" Arthur asked, having difficulty keeping his attention on the road ahead.

"They've been to the Hall twice. How they are treating Violet, I don't know," she answered honestly. "She does not confide in me."

Arthur seemed to nod absentmindedly, his grip on the reins loose, his gaze unfocused. "Does she have someone assisting her?" he asked following a few moments of quiet.

"Someone to help navigate them and their interviews?"

"I suppose Benson, the estate manager, has been available, but I don't think Violet is the sort to lean on others too much. She keeps to herself, you understand. She's very independent that way."

A quick laugh escaped him, a breath caught as soon as it was released. "Don't I know it."

They rounded a bend and the Hall came into view in the distance. The direct view of the building was marred by a stand of trees, naked and spindly. The snow covering the surrounding fields no longer shined pristine white as it had after the storm. Now the landscape looked grey, the snow mounds jagged, the stone wall and building exterior like thick blocks of ice chiseled haphazardly without any regard to shape or form. As the carriage drew closer, Margaret noticed there was something different about Wendall Hall that day. No longer did it look inviting, an oasis of warmth in a desert of ice, but rather it stood like a tomb, boxed, sealed, and barring any entry or exit. Any joy she once had in arriving at work was now gone. The memory of stumbling over the body two days prior, the cascade of emotions she experienced, and the relationships it had strained sat heavily on her chest as Arthur brought the sleigh to a halt in his usual spot.

Margaret sat for a moment longer looking up the drive, trying to ignore a dry feeling in her gut, the feeling that told her that day wouldn't be a joyous one. When she looked back to Arthur to give her daily thanks she saw the look of longing on his face, a look of familiarity and confusion. A pained expression, as if holding back a truth that demanded to be said.

For the first time Margaret considered the possibility that Arthur may have had a connection to the place, perhaps even a connection to Violet Bane herself for some act of kindness or generosity he wasn't yet willing to share. Such a connection would explain his willingness to assist Margaret in getting to work every day, his support of the charity work performed there, especially in a town so bent on discrediting the necessity of a women's health institution. Arthur's support had been an anomaly and Margaret had only begun to understand why.

"I'm sure Violet would love to see a friendly face," Margaret ventured, "especially at this trying time."

Her words broke him from his reverie and brought his attention away from the building and back to Margaret beside him. "Will you deliver a message for me?" he asked.

Margaret twisted in her seat to regard him squarely. "Why can you not bring your message to her yourself?"

Arthur gave an awkward smile and shook his head, the idea preposterous. "I don't think she'd appreciate that," he said.

"If she behaves horridly you can blame me. You can tell her I put you up to it. I'm almost certain she hates me."

"Oh, I don't know 'bout that," he said, without bothering to qualify whether he meant he wouldn't come inside or whether Violet hated Margaret. "Just, tell her I've been thinking of her. And"—he drew a steadying breath—"and tell her if she ever needs anything all she needs to do is ask. Can you do that for me?"

"Of course." It had become clear Arthur would not leave the sleigh, no matter how much Margaret coached him. Without a thought, Margaret leaned in and planted a kiss on his exposed cheek and smiled. "Have a good day, Arthur."

He tipped the brim of his hat. "You as well, Mrs. Davies."

The sleigh bells chimed merrily, signaling his departure as Margaret began her steady walk up the drive. She held her breath as she skirted the spot where Emma's body was found and hurried inside. The door groaned against the ice on its hinges and the wood floorboards beneath Margaret's feet called out a matched tune. In the cloakroom, Margaret removed her scarf and coat slowly, lost in thought. She knew she should go to Violet first. The day prior she hadn't spoken to Violet much at all, let alone acknowledge the sore feelings between them. If experience had taught her anything it was to never leave off for tomorrow what could be addressed and rectified that day.

Margaret gave a gentle rap on Violet's closed office door and waited. There was a chance she was with a patient upstairs in one of the rooms but Margaret heard shuffling beyond the door when she first entered the building.

"Come in," Violet called, a few seconds after Margaret's

knock.

Margaret forged ahead. "Good morning, Violet," she said. "I just wanted to let you know I am here—"

With the door open, Margaret could see Violet was not alone. Seated in the chair before the large desk sat Mrs. Campbell, who turned slightly to face Margaret as she entered. The woman's eyes bore into her, slits of royal blue blotched by what must have been hours of crying.

"Margaret, I believe you've already met Mrs. Campbell," Violet said, circling her desk.

"How do you do, ma'am?" Margaret asked, unable to think of anything less mundane or trivial.

Mrs. Campbell merely forced a tiny smile and then lifted her handkerchief to her nose, half hiding her face.

"Mrs. Campbell and I have been talking about her daughter and Fannie Mae," Violet explained.

"Yes, of course." Margaret could see the weight of the conversation in Violet's posture. It was a sad business for all involved, Margaret realized, saddest for Mrs. Campbell, who had lost her adopted child, and equally as difficult for Mrs. Bane, who had facilitated the adoption. "I won't bother you further," Margaret said, pulling the door back as she made her retreat.

"Margaret?"

She stopped with the door halfway closed and raised her gaze to Violet, who looked at her expectantly.

"I would very much like to speak with you," Violet said. "Perhaps I may come find you once my work with Mrs. Campbell is finished?" She seemed to be asking, without expectation, an apology hidden among her tone.

Margaret gave a slight nod and pulled the door to a close.

She found Mrs. Gibson in the kitchens, helping Cook roll out pastry dough at the long preparation counter. Numerous empty pie shells lined the table waiting for their filling and it looked as if the women had many more to roll out before they would be through. A welcome smile appeared on Mrs. Gibson's face once she saw Margaret.

"Oh, thank goodness," she said, turning to face her squarely. "Room 207 has been asking fer ye since I arrived two hours ago," she said. "She looks nice enough, but that young lady would not take no for an answer."

"Is something the matter?" Margaret asked, shifting her gaze from Mrs. Gibson to Cook and back again.

Both women seemed to exhale in unison, dropping their shoulders as they did so. "The only thing the matter is her lack of patience," Mrs. Gibson said.

Margaret felt the presence of someone behind her. When she looked she saw Fannie Mae, her jaw tight and her chin slightly elevated. She moved farther into the room as if intent to keep as much distance between her and Margaret as possible.

"Good morning, Fannie Mae," Margaret said, perhaps a little desperately. As soon as she said it she knew she shouldn't have bothered. Fannie Mae kept her gaze on Mrs. Gibson, acting as if Margaret weren't even there.

"I didn't expect you to be coming today," Cook said, "on account of what's happened to yer sister and all."

"I'm waiting for Mrs. Campbell," Fannie Mae said, drawing close to the centre work table. "She and I are going to town to pick up a dress. It had been ordered and fitted for Emma. Mrs. Campbell said it was best if I were to have it."

"That's nice of her," Mrs. Gibson said, darting her eyes to Margaret.

The tension between all of them was palpable. Their words punctuated, their gazes unfocused, as if everyone had some place else they'd rather be.

"How is Mrs. Campbell?" Margaret asked, suddenly finding the strength to ignore Fannie Mae's dismissive treatment of her. "I saw her just now in Violet's office. She doesn't look well."

"She's lost her child, Mrs. Davies," Fannie Mae said, releasing a breath as if it pained her. "I'd say she's doing rather well given the circumstances." She did not move her head or shift her gaze. Instead, Fannie Mae kept her eyes trained on the large sheet of pie pastry being rolled out in front of her. "Is there some tea ready?" she asked.

Mrs. Gibson gestured toward the far counter with a nod of her head, her hands full. Her eyes went straight to Margaret, as if surprised by Fannie Mae's sudden cold shoulder toward her.

Margaret had dealt with things like this growing up but

never to this extent. She was taught at home by either her mother, and later her governess, so was never truly subjected to the onslaught of in-favour-out-of-favour antics young girls are known for. She had heard of the games and taunting often used to disarm those who were thought to be inferior. It was something girls never really seemed to grow out of. Margaret had seen her mother treated in a similar way. She had been excluded from society, an outcast for a myriad of reasons that all seemed to have stemmed from being thought either too wealthy or not wealthy enough. It was a game in which, once someone decided they did not like you, you were never going to win.

"I'll see to Room 207 now, Mrs. Gibson," Margaret said, no longer willing to subject herself to Fannie Mae's poor treatment. "You'll find me there if you need me."

Chapter 18

Bethany was hunched over the foot of her bed, using the wooden structure to keep herself upright, as Margaret entered.

"I can't do this anymore," Bethany said.

"What's the matter?" Margaret rushed to her side.

"Get this thing out of me," Bethany answered, moving her grip to Margaret.

"Are you experiencing contractions?"

"What are contractions?"

"Pain that comes and goes at regular intervals. You mostly feel it in your back."

"Yes, yes. I feel pain in my back." Bethany waved her hand dismissively and then clung to Margaret as if she were the only thing holding her upright. Her face was scrunched up as if in pain and her eyes closed.

"How many minutes pass between them?" Margaret asked, allowing Bethany to brace herself completely on her.

"There's nothing," Bethany said, breathlessly. "It's constant. Oh, Margaret, make it stop. I just want this over. Get it out of me."

"Everything is going to be all right." Margaret guided her toward the side of the bed. "When did Ms. Violet tell you the baby would arrive?"

"She said I had a couple days, but Aunt Jane wants it over before Christmas."

"Your aunt doesn't get a say," Margaret said. She set Bethany down on the edge of the bed, and helped her climb on top of the covers. "I'm going to have to check to see how far along you are," Margaret said. "If the head is crowning I have to call for Ms. Violet."

"Yes, all right," Bethany hissed. "Oh dear God, Margaret, I just want this over. Please tell me it's almost over."

Margaret took a quick peek and pulled back Bethany's nightdress to nearer her knees.

"What? What is it?" Bethany asked.

Margaret moved around the bed and placed a hand on Bethany's stomach and the other on Bethany's back. After a few seconds of waiting, Bethany tensed up on the edge of panic, Margaret pulled her hands away. "You aren't in labour."

Bethany looked to Margaret in disbelief for a few moments before she threw her head back into the pillows and covered her face as if to cry.

"I'm sorry, Bethany, but you are just as you were yesterday—in your final days and very near the end, but this baby is not ready to come out."

"But it must come out," Bethany said, reaching over and grabbing Margaret by the arm. "You must be able to give me something to hurry things along, a medicine, an antidote."

"You are too far along for any antidote." Margaret smiled, finally seeing the real reason for her friend's panic. Bethany was most likely in near-constant discomfort. Her ankles were swollen, her chest short of breath. Margaret had no doubt she had trouble sleeping. This was the nature of pregnancy, the final stages Margaret herself was not looking forward to.

"Can't Ms. Violet cut it out?" Bethany asked, making a slicing motion with her hand across her pregnant mound. "I've heard of them doing that sometimes."

"Which almost assuredly means death for the mother," Margaret pointed out.

Bethany was unaffected by Margaret's mention of the outcome. She merely shrugged. "Wouldn't be any worse than what is waiting for me back home," she said.

Margaret leaned up against the edge of the bed and took up Bethany's hand. "You said no one knows but your aunt."

"I think Father knows."

"What makes you say that?"

"Just the way Father was looking at me the day we left. I had been so careful to hide it but perhaps we left on our journey a little too late. It's been months since I've been home so I've had a lot of time to think about it," Bethany confessed. Her gaze grew distant, only half focused on the coverlet of the bed. "Yes, I think he knows."

"Will he tell your mother?"

"I don't think so. If he did, she'd certainly blame him and he'd blame her and around and around we'd go." Bethany was speaking with an air of resignation. "I promised my aunt we'd be back by Christmas—"

"I don't think that's possible," Margaret said. "Christmas is three days away. Unless this baby decides to come right this minute the chances of you recovering and making the journey in time is very small."

"But there must be something we can do," Bethany pleaded. "Perhaps a long walk or bring me a horse and I'll go for a ride. That aught to do the trick."

Margaret laughed. "Or we could wait. Waiting won't cause injury to the child or to yourself."

"Of course you would say that," Bethany said. "You were always the good one."

"I'm not entirely good."

"Oh, but you are. Of all the people I have ever met you are by far the most kind and considerate, if perhaps a bit docile."

"Come now!"

A giggle escaped Bethany and then just as suddenly her expression turned serious and she eyed Margaret in a peculiar way. "I can think of none better to ask but you."

Margaret was confused. "Ask me what exactly?"

Bethany took a moment, and shifted her gaze. "Will you and Jonas adopt my baby?"

Margaret sat dumbfounded for a moment. Her hand went to her stomach. "Bethany, I'm with child."

"So much the better. It's not as if you never intended to start a family. What's the matter with starting your family a few months earlier?" Bethany paused and waited for a reply. "I suspect giving up my baby will be the hardest thing I will ever have to endure. I want to know that he or she goes to a family who will love them and care for them."

"Jonas and I are not well situated," Margaret said. "Mrs. Bane may be able to find your child a match with a nobleman's family, someone in a higher social class than a surgeon."

"Wealth and property does not equate to love and guidance, you of anyone knows this, Margaret," Bethany pointed out. "It matters more to me that my child is part of a loving family, whether they be rich or poor. Besides, knowing they are in your capable hands will afford me the opportunity to check in once in a while."

"Mrs. Bane says even occasional contact can make the heartache worse, not better."

"Mrs. Bane doesn't know me very well then," Bethany said. "I feel I would die from not knowing." She snatched up Margaret's hand and held it in both of hers. "I promise, if you and Dr. Davies agree, I will sign over all parental rights and never speak of it again. You have my word. I should only like to be known as Aunt Bethany so I may shower them, and your other children, with gifts and affection. I will die an old maid, I am sure of that now and, if you agree to raise my child as your own, you will give me some measure of happiness between now and then."

"I wish you wouldn't speak so solemnly," Margaret said. "My wish is for you to find a kind-hearted man, one who will love you as Jonas loves me. How do you know you won't wish to take back your child and raise them alongside your others?"

Bethany huffed. "As if many men would be so willing to provide for a child not their own." She shook her head. "I fear you do not know the gold you struck when you chose Jonas as your husband. He is unlike other men of our time, very unlike them indeed."

Margaret smiled. She knew this, and yet perhaps Bethany was right; Margaret didn't fully appreciate the scope of her good fortune. "Bethany, I—"

A loud *THUNK!* sounded somewhere in another part of the building. At first, Margaret wasn't sure if it hadn't just been something she had heard, but when her eyes met Bethany's she could tell she had heard it as well.

"What was that?" Bethany asked.

Margaret didn't reply. Instead, she listened intently and heard the faint sounds of a person yelling, perhaps two people arguing. "Stay here," Margaret cautioned, as she rose to her feet and went for the door. "I'll see what is the matter."

In the hall she could hear the commotion ever louder and determined it was coming from the first floor.

"Get that thing away from me!" Benson's voiced boomed from the storey beneath her.

A curious patient poked her head out a door across the hall, her face as equally alarmed as it was intrigued. Margaret pulled Bethany's door closed and made for the stairs.

"What's going on?" the patient asked, allowing half her body to remain obscured by the door frame as she pulled her dressing gown tighter around her midsection.

"It's all right," Margaret said. "No harm will come to you. Stay in your room."

The patient did as she was bid and allowed Margaret to pull the door closed.

"I ain't done nothin' to ye!" Benson bellowed. A loud bang rang out, the sound of wood, a chair perhaps hitting the floor.

Margaret surveyed the hall for others and, seeing none, she made her way down the stairs. Mrs. Gibson stood at the doorway of the nursery, a small bundle, a newborn, in her arms. When she saw Margaret she nodded to where the commotion was but would not venture out. "The dining hall," she said in a whisper.

"It was ye who did it!" Mrs. Campbell's voice came to Margaret as loud as if she had been standing right in front of her. By the time Margaret made it to the dining hall she found Mrs. Campbell with her back to the hearth, the long black iron poker stretched out in front of her at its full length, the pointed edge directed at a cowering Mr. Benson, who had been backed into a corner. An evergreen tree lay on the floor, overturned with many of its needles scattered over the floor.

"Fannie Mae told me everything!" Mrs. Campbell yelled, oblivious to all others in the room. "You killed her. You killed my baby!"

"I did not." Benson stood behind an overturned chair, his exit blocked by the long utilitarian dining table now askew. He moved to push the table out of the way but Mrs. Campbell lurched forward brandishing her weapon and forcing him back again.

Fannie Mae stood back from the immediate row, her expression one of alarm and almost fear. Her features changed, however, as soon as her gaze met Margaret's to something more resembling defiance.

"Do something," Margaret urged. "Stop this. Do not tell me you believe Benson capable."

Fannie Mae shook her head slightly and made no indication she would move. Violet rushed into the room, stopping abruptly at Margaret's side, barely a step into the door.

"Mrs. Campbell. Stop this at once!" she ordered.

The grieving mother narrowed her gaze and paused her progress but did not lower the fire poker. "How can you employ such a monster?" she asked, without bothering to look in Violet's direction. "And in such proximity to children!"

"Nothing of the sort has been proven," Violet said. "Mrs. Campbell, if you do not lower that poker I will be forced to summon the police."

Mrs. Campbell finally turned her gaze. "And what will they do? Arrest a grieving mother?"

"If need be," Violet said without hesitation. "And I will ask you to leave this facility and never return."

Mrs. Campbell turned, lowering her iron implement and allowing it to dangle at her side. "Spoken like the childless woman you are," she said. "What would you know about being a mother? What do you know of my grief?"

With just a handful of words Violet's composure was lost. Her eyes spilled over with tears and her chin trembled, revealing a deep pain, but she held her ground, perhaps her suffering reinforcing her resolve. Margaret stepped forward, afraid Violet might collapse. The head matron's grasp was weak in Margaret's hand but she would not move from her spot.

"I grieve just as much as you, Mrs. Campbell," Violet said with determination. "You are not the only grieving mother in this room. I too lost a child. I lost both my girls once, and now I only have one left." Violet's gaze turned to the corner where Fannie Mae stood. Seconds passed before Violet's true meaning dawned on her and, without warning, Fannie Mae collapsed to the floor.

Chapter 19

The roads in Edinburgh were sloppy as the temperature warmed, causing all the snow and ice to melt just enough to create great swaths of water and slush, the sort that was easily sopped up by trouser hems and sloshed over the higher edges of shoes. By the time Jonas walked through the doors of the telegraph office his feet were soaked through and he feared he was well on his way to catching a chill. The line was short, thank goodness, as Jonas was running late. He hurriedly transcribed his message destined for London and left the change to pay for it on the counter, waving good day to the operator as he left.

As usual, no one greeted him as he entered the university building where he worked. His presence was ignored by all who passed. This did not prevent them from staring, though, as they often did as he made his way through the halls. Students would whisper as he went past and his teaching colleagues were hardly any better. Anything said to him while on the school grounds was done strictly out of necessity, and nothing more. No one wished to associate themselves with a once-accused murderer. It did not matter that he had been cleared of all charges, or that he and Peter had hunted down the true killer. In the eyes of everyone around him, Jonas was a marked man and would remain so as long as he worked out of the university.

Dr. John Cameron knew none of this, however, and proceeded to wave and call out to him from the closed door of Jonas's office. "Dr. Davies," he said, bridging the distance between them in a few steps.

Jonas was startled to find such a warm, exuberant greeting. The experience of it nearly warmed him from head to toe.

"I decided to come deliver my findings to you in person," Dr. Cameron said, switching his satchel from one hand to the other before shaking Jonas's hand. "Your colleagues told me you wouldn't be but a minute. May we speak in your office?"

"Yes, of course."

Dr. Cameron filed through Jonas's doorway unaware of the spectacle he had just created for himself. Jonas was very much aware, however, and resisted the urge to glance to all the interested onlookers who had stopped their morning routines to gaze upon the one and only visitor Jonas had had in months.

"I took extra care with the deceased young lady," Dr. Cameron began, as Jonas took his seat behind his desk. Cameron pulled out a single sheet of paper and placed it on the desk between them. "Your eye for detail has me intrigued, Dr. Davies," Cameron said teasingly. "I provided a thorough examination and agree with your original remarks. She was dispatched by a repeated blow to the head, two points of contact. Facial contusions and bruising support your theory that she was already on the ground when the second blow was struck." Dr. Cameron pointed to a few lines of his report to emphasize his point.

Then he pulled a second sheet of paper from his satchel. On this sheet was a standard medical drawing, the outline of an anatomical human being with notes, arrows, and small sketches to indicate precise locations of wounds or discoveries.

"I also found a number of anomalies that may be helpful to the investigation. The woman had a number of bruises over various parts of her body."

Jonas furrowed his eyebrows and leaned in closer for a better look at the drawings.

"Here... and here." Dr. Cameron pointed to her right shoulder and right hip. "These are the most recent, not healed. Probably only a day or so old before the time of her death."

"What sort of bruises?"

Dr. Cameron shook his head. "I can't tell. She may have been hit by something or fallen into something. I spent a lot of time examining them but could not find a definitive cause, nor can I give a likely scenario."

Jonas surveyed the drawing. "And these?" He pointed to a few marks on her legs, including one on her thigh.

"Older bruises, a week old, perhaps a bit longer. They

were definitely further along in the healing process than the ones I just showed you."

"Was she attacked? Forced to..." Jonas hesitated. He hated to think of the possibility, but his search for answers overruled his distaste for it.

Dr. Cameron shook his head. "Her hymen was still intact. She wasn't pregnant nor was there any indication she had been dishonoured."

Jonas nodded and found himself slipping away into his own thoughts. Perhaps the young woman had discovered her origins, or had some suspicions at least. "Anything else I should know about?"

"I found evidence that she had broken both her legs at some point. Not at the same time. One was significantly more healed than the other. And a finger as well."

"How on earth did she receive so many injuries?"

Dr. Cameron shook his head. "Your guess is as good as mine. If she were a male I'd say he's too much a daredevil, but females aren't nearly as driven by risk as that. I find the opposite to be more true actually."

Jonas found himself nodding absentmindedly. His thoughts remained on Emma. It was possible the woman had been subjected to abuse for a considerable amount of time.

"Thank you, Dr. Cameron," Jonas said suddenly. "Have you taken these to Deputy Chief Kelly?"

"I sent it by messenger this morning," he answered. "But I wanted to make the trip into Edinburgh myself."

Jonas raised an eyebrow.

"You see, Doctor, I have always envisioned myself working in Edinburgh, at this very institution," Dr. Cameron explained. "You wouldn't know if there are any openings on the faculty, would you? Perhaps you could put in a good reference on my behalf, considering my thorough job on this matter." The man looked eager, an excitement he quickly tempered once he saw Jonas's hesitation.

"I'm afraid a reference from me wouldn't do much good for you," he explained. "Not at present in any case."

"Oh?"

The enjoyment Jonas experienced with regards to their corroboration was short-lived. He had been relishing the interaction with another doctor, one who supposed them to be of equal footing, perhaps even believing Jonas to be slightly elevated in rank. The reminder that he carried no actual clout or influence brought those feelings tumbling down. Jonas knew he could not continue like this.

"But I have a feeling there will be an opening very soon," he said, gathering up Dr. Cameron's papers.

Dr. Cameron beamed. "Truly?"

"May I keep these?" Jonas asked, nodding to the papers.

"Yes, of course," Dr. Cameron said eagerly. "That was my intention."

Dr. Jonas stood, and Dr. Cameron followed. They shook hands over the desk.

"Thank you, Dr. Cameron," Jonas said, "for all you have done for this investigation. I'm looking forward to repaying the favour. I'll be in touch."

"Yes, yes, of course." The man stumbled slightly, banging into the edge of his chair before making his way to the door. He seemed hesitant to leave but eventually nodded and slipped out into the hall.

Jonas smiled to himself, remembering how eager he had been for his position, any of his previous positions. All of them seemed a step up from the one he had before. For a time, it seemed as if he were making upward progress in his career, like rungs on a ladder, each one higher and more prestigious than the last. Those days were over now, and he doubted he'd ever be able to rekindle the excitement he once had for his work. Something had to change and he knew he was the one who needed to be the catalyst for that change.

Chapter 20

By the time Fannie Mae came around, Mrs. Campbell was long gone. She'd left rather quickly after Violet's confession, no doubt embarrassed by her horrendous outburst. Both Margaret and Violet were too concerned for Fannie Mae's well-being to prevent her from leaving, which was just as well since Mrs. Campbell had made it clear she was in no condition to keep company.

Margaret observed Fannie Mae's eye flutter at first before a gentle moan escaped her lips.

"She's coming 'round," Margaret said. "Quick, fetch a glass of water."

Mrs. Gibson nodded and scurried off into the kitchen.

"Fannie Mae?" Violet held Fannie Mae's head in her lap, both hands cradling her head. "Wake up, dear."

Margaret could tell she was on the verge of crying once more but was forcing herself to remain strong for the crisis in front of them.

Fannie Mae's eyes finally opened slowly and her hand squeezed Margaret's.

"Oh, thank goodness!" Margaret raised Fannie Mae's hand to her lips and gave a gentle kiss, thankful her friend had come around.

Slowly Fannie Mae pulled herself off the ground, allowing both Violet and Margaret to ease her upright. When Mrs. Gibson brought the water she downed half the glass before handing it back. "Thank you," she said quietly.

"Are you all right?" Margaret asked. "Does your head hurt? Did you injure yourself?"

Fannie Mae sat for a moment, as if surveying her pain signals, and then finally shook her head. "Just a bit dizzy," she said.

They helped her to a chair before the fire and Violet moved about to check her pulse and her temperature, and a few other indicators, before finally agreeing to stop fussing. Margaret could hear Violet sniffling as she went about, remnants of her earlier tears, and the torment of admitting to being Fannie Mae and Emma's birth mother.

Sitting in the chair opposite her, Margaret saw Fannie Mae's eyes widen as if suddenly remembering the cause of her collapse. Her gaze went to Violet, who hovered above them. "You are my birth mother?"

Margaret watched as a fresh round of tears came forward. Violet nodded and half sat, half fell into the chair behind her.

"How come you never told me?" Fannie Mae asked, suddenly finding her strength. "I've been working here for three years."

Violet shook her head. "I very nearly didn't hire you. I was so scared of you finding out, but your mother..." Violet cleared her throat. "She came to me and said she hadn't said anything all these years and that you hadn't a clue you were adopted. She begged me not to say anything. As far as I was concerned, my secret was safe."

Margaret saw how Violet's hands trembled. She reached over protectively and gave her a gentle squeeze. Violet smiled at this.

"But my father..." Fannie Mae stammered, as if wanting desperately to know and yet not wanting to know at the same time. "Was he Lord Bane?"

Violet laughed awkwardly, a quick huff and breath at the same time. "No, my husband was over sixty years old by the time we married. I doubt he was even able to sire children by then. He had never had any with his first wife. When he died I was resigned to the fact I would never be a mother and then..." She smiled. "I met a man. We conspired in secret. I was still in my widow's weeds and was expected to mourn a year or longer if I felt the need. But how does one mourn a man one hardly even knows? Losing my husband was not a loss, it was a release."

"But the man, why didn't you marry him?" Mrs. Gibson asked, before giving a look of embarrassment for behaving so boldly.

"Well, he was not a lord or a baron or anything. He was just a man. A simple, wonderful man." Violet shifted uncomfortably in her seat, her heart still affected by the events that had taken place twenty years before. "I called it off. I told him it wasn't acceptable and that I never wanted to see him again. I couldn't trust myself when I was around him and I didn't want to risk anyone finding out." Violet closed her eyes. "And he did as he was told. He left. And a few weeks later I realized I was with child. Two children actually." Her gaze lifted to the room around them. "And so not only were the seeds of life planted but also the seeds of an idea. I wanted to create a place where women could receive care, give birth to their children, and know the adopted families were of moral character. I wanted to provide others with hope where I had none." She looked to Fannie Mae then, reaching though the space that separated them and placing a hand on Fannie Mae's. "I agonized over my decision for years but never more so than in the last few days. I can't help but feel responsible for Emma's death."

Margaret lifted her gaze to Mrs. Gibson briefly, remembering what the nurse had told her on her doorstep. "Emma came here a week ago, didn't she?" Margaret said.

Violet nodded.

"Did she know she was adopted?" Fannie Mae asked.

"Yes, apparently she had ventured to guess and her parents confirmed her suspicion. I'm afraid it hadn't gone over well with Mrs. Campbell."

"Did she know about me?" Fannie Mae asked.

Violet shook her head. "No, dear. When she wrote to me I invited her to stop by on a Sunday, a day I knew you'd not be here. I didn't want to risk you both crossing paths, not until I knew it would be well received and not quite so shocking."

"Did she know you were our mother?"

Violet had a difficult time looking any of them in the eyes. Instead, she focused on her hands twisting and turning in her lap. "No. I had no intentions of ever telling either of you. I started devising a story that I had lost your file or the like. I wanted you both to believe your birth mother was untraceable." She gave a sheepish smile, amused by her hindsight. "Seems foolish now." She wiped a tear from her eye and released a sniffle. "When she came the first time I told her I would look for her file and see what I could discover. I knew she had intended to return but I never dreamed it would be so soon. When I saw her in the snow, I truly did believe it was you, Fannie Mae. I didn't think it possible that Emma had returned, so late in the day as well. I hadn't any inclination that she was coming once again and I still can't fathom why."

"She told the barmaid in Dunbar that evening that she was seeking out her destiny," Margaret said. She looked to Fannie Mae. "When you were outside speaking to Edward, she told me the last time she saw Emma she had a large bag, like she was going on a trip. That bag I found in the Campbells' barn. I think it was Emma's."

If Fannie Mae was intrigued, Violet was shocked.

"What was it doing there?" Violet asked.

"Maybe she changed her mind after the public house and returned home," Fannie Mae suggested, "then for some reason came here without it."

"I doubt it."

Violet touched Margaret's arm to get her attention. "You don't think Mr. Campbell is responsible, do you?"

"I don't know, but I wouldn't put it past him," Margaret said truthfully.

"Where was she planning to go? What was she planning to do with all her items packed in a carpetbag?" Fannie Mae asked.

"She had meant to find her mother," Violet said, closing her eyes at the realization. "She was so determined when we met to find her. She had told me how much she had wanted to find her, how she'd pictured their happy reunion in her mind. I had no desire to disappoint her. To tell her she had already met her birth mother. I bet you she was coming here to demand I tell her where to find her." Violet stood and paced the room. "I should have said something. I should have swallowed my pride and told her it was me." When Violet turned back to look at them her face revealed a renewed round of tears. "I keep thinking of my baby girl on that ground, frozen and cold." Violet squeezed her eyes shut. "I can't sleep without thinking about it, without feeling the chill run up my spine. It's my fault. It's all my fault." Violet burst out into tears. She buried her face in her hands and released a quick succession of wails, sniffling and gasping for breath. "I should have been brave. My little girl died because I was a coward."

"No, Violet," Fannie Mae said. She slid from her chair and walked to her. "It's not your fault. You didn't do this to her. Someone else did. Someone evil and cunning." Fannie Mae turned her face to look at Margaret, a renewed determination in her eyes. "I don't know if it was Mr. Campbell or not, but whoever did this will come to wish they hadn't. Right, Margaret?"

Margaret forced herself to smile. "Yes," she said with a nod. "Yes, they will."

Chapter 21

Jonas was eager to leave work but he couldn't justify a sudden departure only partway through the day. He waited on pins and needles for much of the afternoon before finally ducking out and boarding the first train headed east to Helmsworth that evening. The sun was nearly set by the time he walked through his cottage gate. When he realized Margaret hadn't yet returned home from the Hall he headed for the path through the woods and made his way on foot, cursing the earlier slush that had dampened his shoes and socks.

The urge to reach Margaret had been so strong it propelled him much of the way through the darkened trees. He could still see enough to stay on the path but just barely. Had he come home on a later train he knew he'd have gotten thoroughly lost. With Wendall Hall in his distant sights, through a stand of trees and across the snow-covered clearing, Jonas stopped and looked behind him.

Left behind in his footprints he spied something orange mixed in with the dark, brown soil. Jonas retraced a few steps and knelt down to inspect. Pine needles. Similar to ones he had seen on the bottoms and sides of Emma's boots. He looked down the path from where he had just come. He realized it was Emma's footprint he and Margaret had seen creating a trail through the woods. She had walked this way to get to Wendall Hall on the night she died.

The hairs on his neck rose slowly as his listened to the creaking and groaning of the wood trunks as they swayed in the wind. Something was out there. He could sense someone watching from the darkness. He'd have called out but he knew whoever it was would have already offered a greeting if they wanted their presence to be known. But the woods remained quiet, save for the trees.

Jonas was unnerved. He tightened his grip on his jacket

collar and resumed his direction for the estate. Once in the safety of the lantern light outside the carriage house, he turned and looked again, scanning the field he had just come across, practically running, and scanning the tree line for any sign of the person he knew was out there.

Equally desperate for warmth and knowledge of Margaret's safety, he rushed inside. He shivered one last time as he pulled the door closed and was relieved to find Margaret coming down the hall toward him.

"Jonas." She nearly laughed as she approached. He'd probably have found it amusing were their roles reversed. "What are you doing here?"

"I have the report," he said, fighting a chattering in his teeth.

Margaret looked over her shoulder before guiding him to a nearby room, a storage room with crates and old furniture piled in abject arrangement. He noticed a window on the farthest wall that overlooked the rear field behind the barn and he couldn't help but rush to it.

"What did Dr. Cameron find?" Margaret asked.

"She wasn't with child," he said, allowing Margaret to pull the snowy scarf away from his throat. "She was still a maid."

Margaret wrapped her arms together over her chest and hugged herself. "Mr. Campbell told me that his wife believed she had a sweetheart, but I now think Emma didn't come here because she was in trouble. I think she came here to find her birth mother."

A flutter of movement outside caught Jonas's attention, bringing him back to the window glass.

"Why do you keep looking out there?" Margaret asked, coming to his side.

"Someone was following me," he said, still somewhat breathless from his journey and shaken by his stalker. "They were right behind me the entire way through the woods. I could feel them on my heels, but when I looked I couldn't see anything. Got me thinking of—"

"The night Emma was murdered." Margaret's terrified expression mirrored his own. She stepped back from the window and moved as if to make way for the door, but by this time Jonas had seen what he was looking for, a male figure skirting the carriage house, tracing Jonas's steps through the snow. Jonas went for the door, sidestepping Margaret, and burst out into the side yard. He tore after the man just before he had reached the doors of the barn.

"Stop!" he yelled, and then powered forward, struggling against the snow that slowed his steps.

The figure froze, hesitating, as if contemplating whether to dart left or right. Jonas was a few paces from him when the man lurched to the right, rounded the corner of the carriage house, and began a retreat back into the woods. He was quick and nimble, able to easily make progress while Jonas fought for each of his steps. Jonas made up for the distance on the downhill, halfway between the Hall and the forest, before finally lunging. The pair tumbled down the snowbank, Jonas clinging to the figure while the man struggled to pry himself free. By the time the pair came to a stop, their faces, hair, and clothing were covered completely in snow. Someone was running up behind them.

"Jonas, stop!" Margaret yelled, once she was a few paces from them.

When Jonas looked at the figure, he had a young man by the shoulders, his hands curled into fists with the man's jacket sleeves twisted in his grasp.

"That's Edward, Emma's brother," Margaret said.

It took a moment for Jonas to realize what she had just said. "It was you? You killed your sister?"

The young man looked terrified. "No," he said quickly. "No, I could never do such a thing." He looked incensed, the reality of the accusation hitting him all at once.

Jonas still did not feel comfortable letting him go. "She had bruises, Margaret," Jonas said, without taking his eyes from Edward. "Emma had multiple bruises all over her body. Some as recent as a few days before her death. Others nearly healed over. She had broken bones too."

"Oh, dear God." Margaret raised her hands to her mouth.

"It wasn't me. I'd never hurt her," Edward pleaded, resigned to Jonas's control. "She was my sister. I loved her as I do my little brothers."

Jonas studied his face, seeking a sign of the young man's sincerity.

"Please," Edward begged. "On the night Emma was killed

I was at home, with my brothers. We were singing carols and making paper fans and cones for the tree. You can ask them yourself." He closed his eyes in an effort to steady his breathing. "I am not lying."

Jonas finally relented, pulling him up off the ground and ensuring he was steady on his feet before releasing his grasp. "Why were you following me?"

"I wasn't following you," Edward said, still cautious. "I didn't know who you were." He looked past Jonas to Margaret behind them. "I was coming to Wendall Hall to warn you. You and Fannie Mae seem like such nice people. I don't want you involved in any of this."

When Jonas looked to Margaret he saw her expression soften, a look of realization mixed with sadness. "I know who killed Emma," she said, looking at Jonas. She nodded to Edward. "You'd better come inside," she said, "both of you. I'll make some hot cocoa."

༄ ༅

It took some time before the fire and two mugs of hot cocoa each before Jonas and Edward stopped shivering.

"Your mother is a demanding woman, isn't she, Edward?" Margaret asked, picking up his second empty mug from the table in front of him.

Edward nodded with a far-off look in his eyes. "You can never please her. She expected more from Emma than from any of the rest of us. She'd always been so hard on her. I could never seem to figure out why. And neither could Emma. We learned to accept it. And she told me to stop protecting her. And I soon realized that was her way of protecting me."

Margaret returned to Edward and Jonas's side, and slid into her seat in front of the fire. Fannie Mae and Violet had retired earlier to Violet's suite of rooms, where Margaret imagined they continued to talk and answer questions, making up for a lifetime of missed opportunities.

"Emma found out she was a foundling," Margaret offered.

"Yes, a few months ago. I believe she had been suspicions for a long time and somehow tricked Father into saying something. I don't know exactly. I wasn't there but it seemed like Emma changed overnight after that." Edward hugged his blanket tighter over his shoulders.

"She frequented the public house," Margaret said. "Rebelling against the wishes of your parents."

Edward nodded. "I kept telling her not to. They let her get away with it for a while but then..." His voice trailed off and he released a long sniffle. "Things grew much, much worse. Mother was convinced she had behaved inappropriately. I came home one day and heard her screaming at Emma. She said she'd end up just like her birth mother, damaged and no good to anyone."

Margaret stifled a gasp. She could hardly imagine anyone saying that to their child.

"And what did Emma do?" Jonas asked.

"She left."

"She left?"

"She didn't say goodbye, to any of us. The barmaid at the public house said she had been there and had left. We didn't know where she was."

"And your mother went out looking for her?" Margaret said.

Edward nodded. "Mother and Father. The boys and I were asleep by the time they got home. They were so quiet the next morning I thought they hadn't found her. I was too scared to ask what happened, so I just went to the barn to start—" He didn't finish his sentence. Instead, he buried his face in the blanket.

Margaret could hear his muffled cries, the regret and loss for not having done more to save his sister.

"It's all right, Edward," Margaret said. "You did your best."

"I swear I didn't know," he said, sniffling. "Not until you and Fannie Mae came and told us she had been found. Then I knew and I was too much a coward to say anything. I just wanted everyone to go away. I wanted things to go back to the way they were."

"Of course you did. It's all right."

The room fell silent as the flames in the fireplace licked the edges of the wood.

"If you don't mind me asking, ma'am, but how did you know?" Edward asked. "How do you know I am telling the truth?"

Margaret was reluctant to speak. Her gaze went to Jonas. "One of our patients saw something that night. Originally, she had told me she saw a man by the carriage house but when I took her to the train station she told me she had heard arguing between two people. She thought it had been coming from inside the building but it's more likely the noise came from outside her window. The station was so loud and busy she was forced to board the train before she could tell me exactly what she saw. She wrote the words 'namtoon' on the window."

"Namtoon?" Jonas ran the word through his mind, thinking of any variations in pronunciation.

"She was trying to spell 'not man'," Margaret said. "She forgot to write the word backward so I could read it the proper way. She was telling me it wasn't a man she saw."

"She saw a woman hiding near the barn?" Jonas asked.

Margaret nodded. "Emma must have come up the same path you and I had taken home. But before that the patient saw Mrs. Campbell waiting for her near the barn."

"And my father, where was he?"

Margaret shook her head. "I don't know."

The room darkened as the fire dimmed, much of the wood fuel having been consumed while they spoke. It was growing late and Margaret and Jonas could do little about any of it until morning.

"Perhaps I can borrow Mr. Benson's carriage for the night," Jonas said, removing the blanket from his shoulders and standing up. "I can use it to see Edward home and then come back for you, Margaret."

A look of alarm washed over Edward's face. "I can't go back there," he said. "She'll know I came here. She'll make me regret it."

Jonas and Margaret exchanged a look. "He can't stay here," Margaret said. "No men permitted."

Jonas nodded. "We have a guest bedroom at the cottage," he said. "Perhaps you can spend the night there until we can get everything cleared up."

This arrangement seemed to appease Edward, who nodded somberly. "Thank you," he said, "to you both."

Margaret smiled. "You are a brave young man for coming

and telling us all this," she said.

Edward laughed nervously. "I don't feel so brave."

"Emma would be proud of you," Margaret said. "I know she would."

Chapter 22

With the morning came renewed snow flurries but also an unrelenting wind that pelted Jonas's face with tiny ice crystals as he rode to Haddington. He had borrowed a horse and saddle from Arthur and made sure both Margaret and Edward were safely deposited at Wendall Hall before he set off. Arthur had told him he'd be back in Helmsworth before midday if Jonas needed anything else but that he could keep the horse as long as he had need of it. Jonas couldn't show his appreciation enough for Arthur's help.

"This is about that murdered woman, isn't it?" Arthur had asked.

Jonas managed a nod but didn't wish to reveal more than that.

He set out at a quick pace, ignoring the weather conditions and only thinking of what Edward had revealed to them the evening before. These details must be known to the police. Mrs. Campbell must be held to account for what she had done to that young woman.

The station house was small, smaller than Jonas's and Margaret's cottage altogether, and crowded, overrun with officers in uniform and the general public vying for their attention. Once past the threshold, Jonas inquired after Deputy Chief Kelly at the desk and was directed to the doorway of an adjoining room.

"Deputy Chief Kelly?"

"Yes. Who wishes to know?"

"My name is Dr. Jonas Davies."

"Your wife works at Wendall Hall, doesn't she? You've been taking liberties with my case, Doctor. I'll thank you and your wife not meddle any further—"

"Our meddling has solved the case," Jonas interjected.

Kelly raised an eyebrow, amused yet disbelieving.

"Have you received the report from Dr. Cameron?"

"I received it yesterday but haven't had a chance to look at it. Why?"

Jonas told him everything, starting with the scene Mrs. Campbell had caused at the Hall the day before, relaying the details just as Margaret had described them to him, and ended his tale with Edward's arrival later that evening.

"The boy now believes his parents are responsible?" Kelly looked doubtful but enthralled.

"Yes, it's conceivable they thought Miss Campbell had been with child and out of wedlock. But Dr. Cameron's report states she wasn't, nor had she been improper at any time."

"And the boy cannot account for his parents' whereabouts the evening Miss Emma Campbell was murdered?"

"No, sir, he cannot."

Kelly nodded. "Very well then, looks like we need to pay this family a little visit. Sort some of these details out."

Jonas was on his horse and heading down the road before Chief Deputy Kelly had the opportunity to rally his men. There was an anxiety present in Jonas, something telling him time was of the essence. He needed to get to the Campbells before they realized Edward was gone and the police were on their way.

No one answered at the front door. Peering through the glass of their front window, Jonas could see no movement inside and decided to head around to the back. In the barn he found Mr. Campbell hunched over his workbench, an iron implement, a tool with a blunt end, in his hands.

"Mr. Campbell?"

The man didn't look up from his work. A large wagon wheel lay flat in front of him, the metal ring removed, the bare wood cracked and worn. A new spoke, freshly carved and sanded, sat ready to be set into place.

"Mr. Campbell, where is your wife?" Jonas asked cautiously.

"You're that young woman's husband, aren't you?" he asked, finally taking his eyes from his work. "The doctor."

Jonas nodded but refused to let down his guard. Mr. Campbell's gaze shifted to look over Jonas's shoulders. Jonas could hear the sounds of a wagon pulling up to the front of the house, and then another shortly thereafter. He did not need to look. He knew it was members of the

Haddington police.

"Mr. Campbell, I'd like to ask you a few questions," Deputy Chief Kelly said as he made his way toward them. He was yelling against the roar of the wind that shook the barn doors and rattled the weather-worn boards that made up the building.

Mr. Campbell dropped his tool to the wood table and closed his eyes in resignation. He had known they were coming, Jonas imagined. It had only really been a matter of time.

"What's this about?" Mr. Campbell asked, slyly pulling something from the tabletop and hiding it behind his back as he squared his shoulders to them.

Jonas backed away. "He has something in his hand," he said to Kelly.

"Now, Mr. Campbell, don't do anything rash," Kelly cautioned. He gestured for one of his officers behind him to come to the side. "We only came to speak with you and your wife. Is she in the house?"

"My wife left with my boys earlier this morning," Mr. Campbell said, his chest heaving. "I don't know where she went." His eyes darted between Jonas, Kelly, and the other officers, most likely calculating his ability to take them all on at once. Jonas imagined they'd all get hurt to some extent but Mr. Campbell, by far, would take the brunt of it.

"Where were you on the night your daughter was killed?" Kelly asked.

"I was here," Mr. Campbell said.

"That's not what your son told me," Jonas said.

"Which son? Edward?"

"You were with your wife, weren't you?" Jonas braced himself against the strong winds and ignored the unrelenting snow. "You had followed her to Wendall Hall, or you knew at least that was where she was headed."

The man's eyes darted about, unfocused on various parts of the floor, as Jonas spoke. "Emma was a wicked, wicked girl. We should never 'ave accepted her." He lifted his gaze then, meeting Jonas's squarely. "It's in the blood. Promiscuity is in the blood. She turned out just like her mother and we should have known. We should have seen it."

"Why did you go there, Mr. Campbell?" Kelly asked. "Why did you go to Wendall Hall that night?"

"We went to bring her back," Campbell snapped, his temper shortening. "That's all. I swear to it."

"But you didn't bring her back," Jonas said.

Mr. Campbell's eyes closed. "I didn't know she was going to do that," he said, his mouth turning down and his eyes welling up. "I hadn't realized she had pulled it from the back of the wagon."

Kelly stepped forward, a quizzical look on his face. "Pulled what from the back of the wagon?"

Mr. Campbell pulled his hand out from behind him but before Jonas could see what he held the uniformed officers jumped in to protect their deputy chief. Three officers wrestled Mr. Campbell to the ground and the tool in his hand skidded across the barn floor. Jonas hurried to see what it was. Kelly lingered just behind him.

Gingerly, Jonas used both hands to lift the farm implement from the floor and held it out for Kelly to see. "Freshly cleaned," Jonas noted. "I'd wager an hour ago this had Emma Campbell's blood on it." He looked to Mr. Campbell, who was face down on the floor, two officers holding him in place.

"What's this?" Kelly walked to the corner of the barn and pulled a carpetbag out from a hiding place beneath a table. "It's Emma's," he said, snapping one of the hooks closed and signaling for one of his officers to gather it as evidence.

"You may not have delivered the blow, Mr. Campbell, but you are just as guilty," Jonas said. "You knew what your wife had done and you did nothing to save your daughter's life."

Mr. Campbell looked horrified at Jonas's words. "What's done was done. Ain't nothing I could do to help her."

"Perhaps," Jonas said. "We'll never fully know, will we?"

"Let me ask this again, Mr. Campbell," Kelly said, crouching down in front of the man as the officers brought Campbell up into a seated position. "Where is your wife?"

Campbell's eyes went to Jonas, and then returned to the deputy chief. He kept his lips closed tight and after a few seconds looked away.

159

Chapter 23

The Christmas tree was erected and placed in the corner of the dining hall sometime after Mrs. Campbell's outburst. "It was best to let it sit anyway," Mrs. Gibson said to Margaret that morning. "It gives the branches time to rest."

Everyone was gathering in the dining hall; even some of the patients had ventured down to lend a hand. Benson had brought two crates down from the attic and now everyone was rummaging through, finding previously made ornaments, papers fans, small white candles, red tartan bows and the like, while assessing what else needed to be done.

"Perhaps Edward would like to show us how he and his little brothers make cones," Margaret offered, trying to invite the shy young man into the excitement. His face lit up at her words and she knew immediately her suggestion had done the trick. She beckoned him to come over so he could explain to Cook what they needed.

It wouldn't take long, Margaret realized, with all the staff pitching in. Benson excused himself, saying he was headed out to wrestle up some pine boughs from the woods. "We can put some above the mantel."

"An excellent idea," Violet said, from Margaret's side. Once the caretaker was gone Violet lowered her voice and leaned in closer to Margaret. "I wanted to say thank you, Margaret," she said, "for your help with Fannie Mae yesterday."

Margaret's gaze went to Fannie Mae across the room. She wasn't completely contented as she had been before, but Margaret could see hints of enjoyment on her friend's face.

"And thank you for your discretion," Violet added, her voice even quieter than before.

"Mrs. Bane, I have always believed trust is the lifeblood of any true friendship and I have no intention of changing that. Your secret is safe with me. I will support whatever action you and Fannie Mae deem necessary."

A smile of relief appeared on Violet's lips. "I have disparaged you," she said. "I misread your intentions when you came here. I thought you had come to amuse yourself, but I see now what a giving heart you truly have. Fannie Mae could not have found a truer friend."

Margaret smiled at this but found her heart growing heavy when her thoughts went to Emma and what Mrs. Campbell had done.

"Dr. Davies has gone to the police?" Violet asked.

"Yes. We should hear from him before long. I will rest easier knowing Edward's brothers are safe from harm." Margaret glanced to the door, half expecting Jonas to be standing there with good news. Her heart dropped when she saw Mrs. Campbell standing beneath the threshold, having just stepped in from outside. She twisted her mittens in her hand nervously but her face displayed a warm, misleading smile.

"Mrs. Campbell." As soon as Fannie Mae spoke the words, the excitement of the room fell flat. All eyes went to the woman at the door, some of them remembering what the woman had done the day before, others unsure what the significance was.

As Fannie Mae stepped forward to greet Mrs. Campbell, Margaret resisted the urge to stop her. Fannie Mae had already retired to one of the empty rooms upstairs by the time Edward paid his visit and Margaret hadn't had a chance to tell her what she and Jonas now knew. She suspected Mrs. Campbell was only being kind to Fannie Mae in an effort to absolve her own guilt.

"What are you doing here?" Fannie Mae asked.

Margaret went forward, protective of her friend, if nothing else.

"Oh, I came to see you, dear," Mrs. Campbell said. She stepped back into the hall and away from the crowd who cautiously returned to their previous activities. "I wanted to apologize for my behaviour yesterday," she said, shifting her gaze from Fannie Mae to Margaret and back again. "I've been experiencing a lot of strain lately and I wasn't behaving like myself." She reached over and touched Fannie Mae's hand, an action that made Margaret's insides jump.

Margaret knew this woman was behind Emma's death. She didn't know where Jonas was and immediately her mind went to all the terrible things that could have happened to him on the road to the police station, especially in the storm.

Instinctively, Margaret went to the side door and peered out the small window into the side garden. She saw the Campbells' carriage hitched up to two horses with James and Stephen seated in the back seat and speaking cheerily to each other despite the whipping wind and unrelenting snow.

"Where are you headed, Mrs. Campbell?" Margaret asked, spying two carpetbags in the front seat. "The weather is so terrible. I hardly think it's a good day for travel."

"Oh, I'm just headed to my cousin's in the city," she said, her words trembling slightly. "Just for the afternoon."

"Perhaps you should stay here instead," Margaret suggested.

"Oh no, I couldn't. I really must be going. I just wanted to see Fannie Mae one last time."

Through the small window, Margaret saw Jonas charging up the drive on his borrowed horse. Fannie Mae came up alongside her and peered out as well.

"What's Dr. Davies doing here?" she asked innocently.

Stephen and James watched enraptured from the carriage as Jonas bounded down from the saddle and hurried for the door where Margaret and Fannie Mae stood.

He came in with a plume of snow and closed the door quickly. His nose and cheeks were crimson and he was out of breath.

"Where is she?" he asked.

Margaret turned to gesture down the hall but found it empty. "She was just here."

Jonas barged forward. "It was her. Mr. Campbell didn't know until the deed was done."

"What do you mean, it was her?" Fannie Mae asked. "Margaret?" She looked to Margaret for an explanation but words failed her.

"We must find her," Jonas said hurriedly. "Kelly's on his way with the others." He headed down the hall, glancing in each doorway as he passed. Margaret walked with him, a feeling of panic rising from the pit of her stomach.

"Margaret!" Fannie Mae called. "What's happening?"

Jonas reached the doorway of the dining hall and stopped, his eyes focused on something in the room.

"Fannie Mae, there's something I've been meaning to tell you," Margaret started.

"Look! There!" Jonas pointed to the windows of the dining hall as Mrs. Campbell darted past, scurrying through the snow outside to reach her carriage. "She went out the kitchen door."

Mrs. Gibson watched her as she went and turned back to Margaret. "She's making a run for it."

"Jonas! The children!" Margaret put a trembling hand up to her mouth,

Before she was able to speak the words, Jonas was rushing for the side door. A rush of snow and wind came at them as he opened it. Through the heavy cascade of snow they could see Mrs. Campbell's carriage hurrying down the lane.

"Stay here," Jonas said, before rushing out into the wintry storm.

Margaret closed her eyes, offering a quick prayer for his safety.

"Margaret! Margaret!" A figure appeared on the stairs, a weak and weary Bethany, hunched over the railing. "Margaret, something's wrong. I don't feel so well." The sweat on her brow glistened in the sunlight. Bethany faltered, nearly losing her grip on the railing and falling backward.

"Violet?" Margaret yelled, running for the stairs. "Fannie Mae, quick! Get Violet!"

Chapter 24

Jonas reached his horse within seconds but had a difficult time getting his foot in the stirrup. Once he was safely in the saddle he urged the mare forward, charging down the snow- covered lane and opening into a full-on gallop once he reached the road.

Visibility was nearing nil. Jonas could make out a faint shadow in the distance, the back end of Mrs. Campbell's carriage. Deputy Chief Kelly and his boys were nowhere in sight.

"Come on!" He tapped his heels into the horse's side and leaned into the wind. As he drew near the carriage he spied two heads peeking out from where they cowered on the bench. The boys looked back at him, terrified but hopeful. Jonas was a few feet from the back of the carriage when one of the boys made a move toward the edge of the carriage. The other boy followed. They intended to jump.

"No!" Jonas called, fearing his words were lost to the wind. "It's too dangerous!"

Mrs. Campbell looked over her shoulder and saw Jonas. She snapped the reins over the back of her horse. Jonas saw the carriage pick up speed, pulling deeper into the snowy abyss.

Steadily, his horse galloped, as if instinctively knowing its rider wanted to keep pace with the carriage. Jonas needed to get the boys off that carriage but it was going far too fast. He wasn't sure they would clear the wheels and wouldn't be crushed under the weight of them. With a few more clicks of his heels, he urged the horse forward, planning to come around the side, perhaps getting the boys off one at a time and on to his horse.

A shadow came out of the falling snow. Another team of horses and a sleigh coming up on an adjoining road, the driver unaware. The sound of jingle bells ringing out and growing louder as the sleigh approached. Jonas pulled back on the reins, anticipating a collision. Mrs. Campbell's horse veered to the left, tilting the carriage as the ground beneath the left-hand wheels rose. Then the horse veered right to avoid a wall of the stone bridge, a sudden jerk that overturned the carriage, tossing its occupants into the snow. Somehow, the horses broke free of the wreckage and kept their rampant pace down the road, disappearing from sight, swallowed by the relentless snow.

Jonas jumped from his saddle before his horse had come to a stop. He found the boys, in the snowbank, covered from head to foot. He knelt between them. "Are you all right?" he asked, quickly surveying the child closest to him.

"I'm all right," Stephen said.

A groan escaped his brother, who had landed two feet away. "My arm," he said, emerging from the snow. "I think I hurt my arm."

Behind him, Jonas heard the sleigh driver running up to them. When he turned he saw it was Arthur, shaken by the near miss. "Take the boys," Jonas said. "Put them in your sleigh. Warm them up."

Arthur nodded and ushered them out of the snow.

"Careful," Jonas cautioned. "I think his arm is broken."

With the boys out of harm's way, Jonas pulled himself up from the snow and staggered to his feet. Not far from him was a small hill, a recess carved out of the landscape long ago by the stream that flowed beneath the bridge. Jonas surveyed the overturned carriage briefly before seeing the heap of what remained of Mrs. Campbell. Jonas scurried down the few feet of slippery rocks to reach her. When he lifted her head he saw that her temple had been bashed in on impact. Blood streaked down her face sideways, staining the pristine snow beneath.

Deputy Chief Kelly appeared on the bank above him. "Is she dead?" he asked.

"Yes, sir," Jonas answered, trying to catch his breath. "She's answering for her deeds to God now."

Chapter 25

"It's meconium," Violet said, rushing about Bethany's room, readying her tools for delivery.

Margaret held fast to Bethany's hand as she lay weakened and sweating profusely. "Meconium?"

"It's the first contents of an infant's bowels," Violet explained, sidestepping Mrs. Gibson, who rushed past with a pitcher of warm water. "Its presence means the baby is under distress," she explained, rushing to the water to wash her hands with the carbolic soap. "More water, Mrs. Gibson. As much as you can bring. I need to clean Miss Brundell up as best I can before she delivers."

Mrs. Gibson nodded and hurried from the room.

"Margaret, I'm going to need your help to keep Bethany calm." She looked for Margaret's agreement and then went for her cache of tools.

Using a wet cloth, Margaret wiped Bethany's brow and offered a soothing tone of voice. "Everything is going to be all right, Bethany," she said.

Bethany looked up, exhausted. "I felt the pains," she said, "but I thought it was just another false alarm."

"We'll get you all better in no time," Violet said, positioning herself at the foot of the bed. "Nothing to worry about. Fannie Mae, I need your help cleaning her up a bit."

Fannie Mae nodded and came to Violet's side. "Warm water and some soap. When the baby comes out we need to pay particular attention to his mouth and face. We need to make sure none of this material comes in contact with it and, if it does, we need to wash it straightaway."

Bethany made no indication that she had heard the midwife's instructions. She lay on her back, collapsed into the pillows, writhing in agony, fearful of what torment came next. Margaret had heard Violet's cautions, however, and she was more concerned than ever.

"The baby is breech, Margaret," Violet said, seeing the look on Margaret's face when she brought forth the metal forceps. "Bethany will labour all day without any progress being made. We have to help it along." She turned to Fannie Mae. "Ready?"

Fannie Mae nodded.

Seconds later Bethany was arching her neck and grabbing for the bedstead behind her as if trying to pull herself away.

"Calm, Bethany," Margaret said, trying in vain to allay her friend's fears. "It will all be over soon."

Bethany let out a scream and squeezed Margaret's hand enough to cut off the blood flow. "Make it stop, Margaret! Make it stop. Let me die. Please, just let me die!"

"No." Margaret fought back tears. "I will not let you die. You have to be strong."

"No one cares for me, Margaret," Bethany whimpered. "I've been tossed aside."

"I care for you," Margaret said. She released a sniffle and used her free hand to wipe her eyes. "You can do this, Bethany. I'm here to help you and that baby."

"Say you'll take it. Promise me, whatever happens, you'll provide a good home for my baby if it lives."

Margaret looked down to Violet and Fannie Mae, who worked to get the baby free. It was the largest request anyone had ever asked of her, one that signified a great deal of respect. She feared Bethany had put her on too high a pedestal and that in the end Margaret would only let her down. She worried about Jonas's reaction, as she hadn't had a chance to speak to him. But most of all she thought of Bethany, her dear friend, who knocked on death's door. How could Margaret's last words to her be ones that would most assuredly break her heart.

"Margaret?" Bethany's voice had weakened. "Margaret, please."

All of a sudden, Margaret nodded. "Yes," Margaret said with conviction. "Yes, of course, Bethany."

At once Bethany relaxed and planted a sweaty kiss on the top of Margaret's hand. She smiled weakly and closed her eyes.

"Bethany, Bethany?" Margaret tried to bring her back around. "Wake up, Bethany. You must pay attention. Ms. Violet's going to tell you when to push. You have to be ready. Are you ready?"

With her eyes only partway open Bethany nodded, and repositioned her head on the pillow. Margaret gave a quick nod to Violet. "All right, Miss Bethany," Violet said, readying her grip on her tool. "Next time you feel that urge to push I want you to bear down as hard as you can. All right?"

Bethany nodded and Margaret wiped her forehead again. A few seconds passed before Bethany let out a grunt of discomfort.

"This is it," Violet said. "Get ready, Bethany. Three. Two. One. Push. Push. Push."

Bethany gritted her teeth and pressed her chin to her chest.

"You're doing so good, Bethany," Margaret found herself saying. "Keep pushing."

In that minute, the movements in the room slowed and everyone's voice morphed into a low droning hum as Margaret watched Bethany struggle. Margaret could not feel her hand but knew Bethany clung to it with the force of ten men. Bethany whined through gritted teeth, releasing a throaty wail signifying her struggle. And then she stopped, threw her head back on the pillow, and gasped for breath. "I can't," she whispered. "I can't."

"She's out," Fannie Mae said. When Margaret looked, Violet and Fannie Mae were concentrating on their work behind the sheet propped up by Bethany's knees. The muted wail of a newborn filled the silence.

"It's a girl," Violet said, taking the small, wet, and discoloured bundle to the washbasin. Fannie Mae flanked her with towels ready and next thing Margaret knew Fannie Mae was holding the baby and Violet was back at Bethany's feet. "More water, Mrs. Gibson. We have to clean Ms. Brundell up. We don't want her getting an infection." Violet looked up to gauge her patient's well-being. "How's she doing, Margaret?" she asked. "Is she all right?"

Margaret looked to Bethany and wiped her forehead once again. Bethany smiled between breaths. "She's fine," Margaret said, elation washing over her. "Our patient is tired, but she's just fine."

Chapter 26

Jonas rushed through the side door to find Margaret and tell her the news. Edward was waiting at the bottom of the stairs.

"She's up there," he said, a look of worry and confusion on his face.

Jonas charged forth, taking the steps two at a time, and went for the open door. He saw Violet first and then Bethany in the bed and quickly averted his eyes. "My apologies," he said, "I was looking for Margaret."

"I'm right here," she said, from somewhere in the room.

"You can come in, Doctor," Violet said. "We're all done in here."

When Jonas looked back, Margaret was walking toward him, a bundle in her arms. He couldn't help but smile at the small babe hidden beneath the layers of blanket. "Who's this little one?" he asked.

Margaret's gaze went to Bethany, who lay in a semi-prone position, propped up by a number of pillows. "I haven't had a chance to ask you," Margaret said, "not with everything that's been going on." Her voice sounded hesitant and unsure. "Bethany has asked if we could adopt her child."

Jonas couldn't hide his confusion. "Margaret, my dear..." He looked to her rounded stomach, the birth of their own child only a few months away. "Are you sure you can handle two little ones so close in age?"

Margaret let out a tiny laugh. "No," she said. "I haven't the first clue."

"Babies are like men," Mrs. Gibson said. "Once you've got one figured out it's not that difficult to figure out the others."

Jonas and Margaret laughed. "We can always hire someone to help us, for the first while at least. I'm sure I can ask Peter to send some funds, if that's what you are worried about." Margaret was searching Jonas's face, as if trying to decipher his true feelings on the matter. "I should have asked you before, and not put you on the spot," she said apologetically.

"No, it's not that," he said, trying to steady the flutter of excitement in his chest. "It's..." He looked to Bethany. He couldn't comprehend the gift she was offering him. A child she had nurtured for nine months all while not knowing the baby's fate. Bethany was a young lady, an heiress from a prominent house; surely she had a much more prestigious upbringing in mind for her child and hadn't meant for the babe to go to a doctor with an impoverished past. "Are you sure you want your child raised by someone like me?" he asked.

"I can't think of a better man," Bethany said, her presence weak but her determination unmistakable.

When Jonas looked back to Margaret he could see the hopeful look in her eye, the kind of look that told him she was ready to commit herself completely if only he were in agreement. "All right," he found himself saying. "But only if you agree to let me hold her once in a while."

Margaret beamed as she handed over the child. Once her arms were free she brushed a tear of joy from her lower lid. "What should we name her?" Margaret asked, with a slight sniffle.

"Oh, I don't know," Jonas said, struck by how light the little thing was in his arms. "We haven't even discussed names yet."

"There's plenty of time to pick names," Violet said. "No point in rushing without any thought."

Suddenly, Jonas remembered something he had been planning to tell Violet. "There's someone here to see you," he said.

"To see me?" Violet smiled and looked about the room,

"He said you were close friends for a time and he wanted to know you were well."

The surprise on Violet's face was unmistakable. She flushed pink and then turned white in a matter of seconds. She looked as if she knew who Jonas had been speaking of, perhaps even anticipating his inevitable visit. The midwife, so full of confidence a moment ago, now looked unsure and jittery. Though resigned to it, Violet did not seem adequately prepared.

"He's waiting downstairs if you'd like to say hello," Jonas said. "I can ask him to leave if you'd prefer."

Violet was quick to shake her head. "No, I'll speak with him," she said, her voice trembling somewhat. She moved for the door with slow, careful steps and stopped at the threshold. "Come along, Fannie Mae," she said. "There is someone I would like you to meet."

After a while they left Bethany so she could rest, and Mrs. Gibson took the baby to the nursery so it could sleep. Margaret pulled Jonas into the dining hall, where the final touches were being put on the tree. "Isn't it lovely, Jonas?" she said, sliding her arm into the crook of his elbow.

"Very lovely."

"Don't you think we should have a tree like this, now that we have a little family to celebrate?" She looked up to him happily, giving a slight raise of her chin, so proud of their accomplishments.

"A splendid idea," he said. "I think we should."

The side door opened and Fannie Mae's mother came bristling in, shaking the snow that had accumulated on her coat. "Mrs. Harris." Margaret stepped forward to greet her.

"I heard in the village there was a kerfuffle at the Hall and I came as quickly as I could," she said. She glanced to Jonas and lowered her voice so only Margaret could hear. "Fannie Mae didn't bother to come home last night and I've been worried sick."

Margaret didn't get a chance to reply. Violet's office door opened and Fannie Mae appeared, most likely hearing her mother's voice. "Mama!" she said.

Margaret could see Fannie Mae had been crying.

"Oh goodness, what has happened?" Mrs. Harris asked, coming toward her daughter.

"Nothing," Fannie Mae replied quickly, "Well, actually, something. Something wonderful. Please come in."

Mrs. Harris looked into the room cautiously before stepping in. Margaret could make out Violet near her desk and Arthur not too far from her. He too looked as if he had been crying. Once the door closed, Margaret looked to Jonas in amazement.

"Arthur?"

Jonas opened his arms to embrace her once more. "After all that's happened they deserve a Happy Christmas," he said.

Chapter 27

With the baby in the nearby bassinet, Margaret stood in the kitchen trying to plan what they were to have for a Christmas feast and at the same time figure out what they may need from the shops. Only two days remained and Margaret sincerely hoped she'd be able to throw something together despite being unaided by any hired help and also despite never having done anything similar in her entire life.

As Margaret surveyed the contents of the pantry, Jonas opened the back door and popped his head into the kitchen. "It wasn't easy with all the snow we received," he said, "but I think I found the perfect tree."

Margaret squared her shoulders to him and placed her hands on her hips. "Oh truly?" she said, somewhat doubtful. She could tell when he was playing at her. He may have been a fully grown man but sometimes Margaret could spy the mischievous little boy that still remained in him.

"Oh, yes," he answered, a playful smile on his face. "I think you'll like it. Are you prepared?"

Margaret laughed and clapped her hands together in excitement. It really didn't matter to her in the least what sort of tree he had managed to find so late before the holidays. She just knew she wanted one as soon as she saw the one at Wendall Hall all decorated and ready for Father Christmas.

It took a moment but Jonas was able to wrestle the conifer into the door, using his body to hide it from view until the last possible moment. In one grand gesture he turned, and held it out in one hand at his side. The tree was no more than two feet tall but it had a full set of branches and accompanying needles. His large hand was wrapped around the near top end of the tree as if he held a dead goose by the neck.

"Voila!" he said, puffing out his chest, proud of himself.

Margaret doubled over in laughter, not only at the minuscule tree but also the overly dramatic manner with which her husband had presented it to her.

Jonas's expression fell. "You don't like it?" he asked, still playing.

Margaret shook her head but was still laughing. "No," she said. "It's perfect."

"I thought so. The parlour is only so large, you know," he said. "I imagined it was the perfect little tree for our perfect little family."

Margaret waddled toward him. "Am I expected to be the perfect little wife to complete your perfect little picture?" She pressed into his side, one of her hands at the back of him, the other resting gently on his chest.

"Oh no, of course not. No one can expect to be the perfect wife," he said, pulling a frown. "But you are perfect for me and that's all I care about." He winked, and then bent down low to plant a kiss on her obliging lips. "Come, wife," he said, "show me. Upon which table would you like me to put our Christmas tree?"

Margaret followed him into the parlour and after a moment's thought they decided it was best to go on the table they would pull from the study. Jonas would not hear of her helping. While he worked at the placement of the tree, Margaret returned to the kitchen to wheel in the still nameless baby into the parlour. "We have to name the wee thing at some point," she said. "Seems a shame to keep calling her 'baby' or 'wee one'."

"All right then," Jonas said, finally satisfied with the position of the tree. "Perhaps we should call her Mary on account of the holiday."

Margaret pondered this.

"If she were a boy we'd have no trouble deciding a name for her," he said.

"Why is that?"

"Because he'd be named Jonas, after his dear Papa." Jonas winked.

Margaret chuckled. "I hadn't taken you for the type who wished to create a namesake."

"I imagine you're right. A child should have their own identity. A fresh beginning. Yes?"

Margaret nodded. "Quite right."

A moment passed in which neither of them said anything. Jonas wandered toward the bassinet with soft steps yet eager anticipation.

"But suppose we did follow with tradition slightly," she said.

"Yes?"

"How do you feel about the name Charlotte?" she said. "After my mother. She's been gone for just over a year now. I know she didn't leave that great of an impression at the end but in my youth she was quite the lady, and she made an undeniable impression on me."

Jonas looked down at the child, who had been sleeping for some time and showed no interest in waking any time soon. "Charlotte." The word rolled off his tongue. "Charlotte."

Margaret smiled at the sound of it.

"All right then," he said at last. "I like it." He reached down into the bassinet.

"Don't wake her."

"I'm not going to wake her."

Margaret glanced out the window, her attention caught by the movement of the snow as it started falling again. In the last week Scotland had received more snow than Margaret had seen in her entire lifetime. The locals told her it was fairly atypical for so much snow to accumulate in such a small amount of time. Margaret liked it, though, pristine white, as if washing away the sins of 1868. The wind had died down at least from the day before.

In the front garden she saw something sticking out of the snowbank next to the walkway. "What's that?" she asked, drawing nearer the window.

Margaret went for the door and headed outside without any covering. In the snow sat the ornate cross from the nearby church, finally succumbed to its fate. Margaret plucked it up from the ground and held it out in front of her.

"The cross," she said, looking back to the front door where Jonas now stood. "It must have come off in the storm." She found herself saddened that she'd no longer be able to view it from her bedchamber window. But Jonas wasn't looking at the cross. His attention was fixed on something down the lane. When Margaret looked she saw a group of people walking toward them. Carolers, Margaret thought at first, but then she recognized them.

"Peter!" She dropped the cross in the snow and went for the gate.

Her brother broke away from the rest and rushed forward. Margaret met him halfway and allowed him to scoop her up slightly as they embraced.

"Oh, my apologies," he said, pulling back and gesturing to her stomach. "I didn't hurt the little one, did I?"

Margaret laughed and ran a hand over her stomach. "No. I'm so glad to see you! You came all this way from London?"

"We had meant to arrive last evening but the snow delayed our progress," he said. By the time he turned back to the group still making their way toward them Margaret could see all who had accompanied him. Aunt Louisa, and all three of her boys, Nathaniel, Hubert, and George. And then Cassandra, Peter's fiancée, holding Peter's adopted daughter, Lucy. Margaret raised both hands to the sides of her face in shock and delight.

"You've come to spend Christmas in Scotland!" she said.

"Yes, my dear," Aunt Louisa said as if it were a forgone conclusion and needn't be fussed over. As Aunt Louisa pulled away, her eyes went from the cottage to Margaret's stomach. "My goodness, Margaret, you're bigger than the house. Which isn't all that difficult, I suppose."

Margaret pressed her lips together to prevent her from saying anything. She hugged her cousins each in turn, and then gave Cassandra a kiss on the cheek. "I hadn't been expecting this. What convinced you all to come?"

Cassandra and Peter exchanged knowing smiles. "It was a telegram from Jonas," Cassandra said.

Margaret turned and saw Jonas standing next to the front door of their cottage welcoming everyone with open arms. "You wrote them?" Margaret asked, walking up the walkway toward him.

"Yes, of course. You said you were homesick. I couldn't bring you to London, so I thought I could convince the best parts of London to come to you." Jonas smiled at Aunt Louisa, who stood waiting beside him.

"Now there's a good husband for you," she said, proud as if she had married him herself. "Come, boys, let us see what sort of a home cousin Margaret has made for herself."

"I can't believe you never said anything," Margaret said, coming to husband's side.

"Well, to be fair, we were both a little busy," he said.

True enough, Margaret thought. True enough.

"Who is this?" Aunt Louisa returned to the front door, took in Margaret's six-month pregnant stomach, and then returned to the parlour. "Who *is* this? Margaret, my dear, I think you have some explaining to do. Yes, this is definitely from your mother's side of the family because I have never seen the like."

Epilogue

Margaret was washing baby bottles and Jonas was sweeping a pile of dust out the back door when Peter entered the room. Christmas had come and gone two days prior and everyone was planning to head out tobogganing later in the afternoon.

"Well, now that I have you two alone," Peter started, sliding his hands into his trouser pockets, "I suppose it's best I come out and tell you both what I have been keeping to myself the last few days."

Margaret lowered the cloth and glass bottle in her hands and steeled herself. When her brother spoke in such tones it was either stupendously good or outrageously bad, and she wasn't about to be caught off guard for either.

"I've spoken with Daniel—well, that is to say I've met with him a number of times, and I've convinced him to forward you your portion of your inheritance."

Margaret looked to Jonas. Shock was not an adequate description. Bewilderment, perhaps, mixed with equal parts disbelief.

"It seems he's been convinced that you aren't completely out of your mind and that, perhaps, it would be wrong to willingly withhold it from you."

"Peter, please be serious."

"I am serious," he said. "It's yours. All of it. He can't keep it from you, even if he disagrees with your choice of life partner." Peter finally cracked a smile, knowing this was the sort of news Margaret had been hoping to hear since the death of their father a month earlier. "Happy Christmas, Margaret."

Margaret's breath caught. She pitched forward and used the chair at the table in front of her to hold herself upright.

"How much are we talking about?" Jonas asked.

"I don't know exact figures," Peter said, "but it's safe to say you and Margaret, if you approach things wisely, will never want for anything ever again in your entire lives."

"Jonas, can you believe it?" Margaret asked, covering her mouth. "I never thought Daniel would relent. I thought my connection to the Marshalls was at an end. I didn't believe I had any claim to the money."

Peter smiled. "And that, dear Margaret, is how I know you will use it wisely."

Margaret turned and found Jonas at her side. She hugged him excitedly and took a deep breath to calm herself. "Jonas, husband, I want us to take this money and do something."

"Margaret..."

"We will put much away of course, for the children, and other things, but in the end the only thing I truly care about is your happiness. Are you happy in your position with the university?"

Jonas's gaze went to Peter, his face confirming what Margaret had known all along. "Actually, I've been thinking," he said. "Oh dear, it's like I could sense this coming to pass but..." He paused to gather his courage. "I've been thinking of returning to London and opening an anatomy school."

"An anatomy school?"

"Yes, Margaret, think of it, a school where anyone can attend, male or female. We can train the next generation of doctors and surgeons, midwives and scientists."

"Female?"

Jonas nodded. "Yes, of course. And we would be closer to your family. You wouldn't have to miss London anymore."

Margaret could feel her cheeks flush with excitement. "We can go back to London."

"Whatever will make you happy, my love."

"But, Jonas, I am happy," she said. "I am so very happy because I have you."

For the next hour Jonas, Margaret, and Peter sat at their kitchen table dreaming up their future anatomy school, a place for both genders and all levels of income. They'd hold seminars and exhibits. They provide lectures and facilitate examinations. It all sounded so wonderful, so much so that as Margaret listened to her husband's and brother's dreams for the future she wondered how it came to be that she had been so fortunate to have such an amazing family.

A Note from the Author

I wanted to take this opportunity to thank you for purchasing and reading my book. I truly hope it was an enjoyable read. At this time I ask you to consider taking a few minutes of your time to leave a review. Whether on Amazon, Goodreads or simply by recommending this book to a friend, reviews are the best way to tip an author and it encourages us to continue writing the characters you love.

I would also like to take a moment to wish all my readers a very Merry Christmas and prosperous New Year.

About Tracy L. Ward

A former journalist and graduate from Humber College's School for Writers, Tracy L. Ward has been hard at work developing her favourite protagonist, Peter Ainsley, and chronicling his adventures as a morgue surgeon in Victorian England. She is currently working on a new mystery series. To find out more about Tracy's books follow her on www.facebook.com/TracyWard.Author or visit her website at www.gothicmysterywriter.blogspot.com

Made in the USA
Columbia, SC
22 September 2018